CIDER

SILVER SKATES

ASPEN BLACK

Editing: Dani Black

Cover: J.E. Cluney

❀ Created with Vellum

ACKNOWLEDGMENTS

I want to thank Jenn for how supportive she's been through this process. It was fun collaborating our books together!

Thank you to my beta readers for their hard work!

Thank you, readers, for supporting Silver Springs once again and enjoying our books!

CHAPTER 1

"Cider, if you don't get up, I'm going to eat your damn blanket and pee in all of your shoes!" Billy leaned in my doorway, his large frame blocking the light as I scrunched my eyes. "Your alarm has gone off for the past hour."

"Fuck off, goat face." I buried my head under the pillow. "I still have thirty minutes until I have to get up."

A sudden dip on the bed had me rolling over. Billy yanked the pillow away from me and I hissed at him.

"Woman, watch who you're spatting at. You have twenty minutes until you're supposed to open."

I jerked upright. "What!? No, it's only six thirty!" I ran my hands through my hair, yanking on the tangles. "Why didn't you wake me up sooner?" Blankets were thrown aside as I scrambled out of the bed and dove across the hallway into the bathroom.

"I'm not your keeper. I'm your roommate." Billy's voice carried through the door. "And I did try. It's not my fault that you snore like Genghis Khan on steroids."

My brush got stuck for a second as I fought it. "That

doesn't even make sense." I decided to stop fighting my hair and just put it up in a bun. My teeth were cleaned, antiperspirant layered on, and all that was needed was clothes. If I was quick, I'd make it in time to open without being late.

"Your face doesn't make sense, but you don't see me complaining." Billy had moved to the kitchen as I threw on clothes. "Your tea is ready."

My smart ass remark stopped at that. He really was the best friend and roommate a girl could have. I'd barely zipped up my jeans when I went into the kitchen.

Billy stood at the stove with his back to me. His shorts hung low on his waist and his back muscles flexed as he flipped the pancake in the pan.

My best friend was hot with his 'dad bod', I think that's what it was called nowadays. Even if he was a goat. And a vegetarian.

My fox turned up her nose at the reminder that people chose not to eat meat. I silently reminded her that we more than made up for him as I patted my stomach.

"Thanks, Billy." I grabbed the thermos on the island. "You really are the best. I'll see you later tonight."

He waved the spatula as I ran out the door to my car. I had ten minutes. If I ignored the street laws, I could make it in five.

My fox wrapped her tail around herself. Big baby. I wasn't that bad of a driver. She disagreed as I zoned her out.

Lucky for me, there had been no police cars around. I made it to my shop with a minute to spare. I punched the air in victory as I flipped the sign to open.

Hot Cider's Beverage and Snack Bar had been a dream of mine since I was a kid. When the Silver Skates Ice Rink popped up, I quit my job, got a loan, and opened up my shop.

The cute little store was decorated for winter with pictures of snowflakes and skates around the walls. There was just enough room for a few tables and chairs. I had a small table outside, too.

I didn't offer hot food, except popcorn and a few candies. But what most people came for were the drinks. Alcoholic and nonalcoholic.

The most popular drink was my Hot Cider's Original. The recipe was secret, but it was my pride and joy. Hot cider mixed with rum, bourbon, cinnamon, a cinnamon stick, apple liquor, and an orange slice. Plus, my little twist on it.

I liked to think that it was the best drink at the rink. Even better than anything Triple E, the shop directly across the rink from mine, could come up with. Triple E and Hot Cider's were rival shops.

At least, that's what I firmly believed until last week. You borrow a set of cups one time, not return them because your abusive ex-boyfriend broke them, and all hell breaks loose.

We'd been in a prank war against each other and the pranks had been steadily escalating. I'd like to think I'd won it, considering Eirlys ended up having glitter orgasms with the side effect of turning my brother's dick blue in the process. Like literally blue. Blue balls probably too.

Quinten still wasn't talking to me. It's not like I'd known he was going to be her mate. Or the one who would end up getting the blue dick. I wasn't thrilled that his mate was Eirlys, especially with the prank war and her being my mortal enemy. You know, all that jazz.

Yet, in the middle of our fighting, Eirlys was kind to me

when she'd found me crying over my ex-boyfriend. She'd given me some encouraging words. Now, we were on an unspoken truce. For how long, I didn't know.

I shook my head. There would be time later to contemplate that aspect of my life. Right now, I had a store to open and customers to feed. After work, I had planned to go skating for a little bit. I wasn't the most graceful skater, but I loved the speed. My fox wanted to learn some tricks, but moving fast was about all I was willing to do for now. My rolls helped cushion when I fell, but if I got seriously hurt, I didn't have anyone to run the store for that long. My part time worker wouldn't be able to handle it.

Since it was the middle of the week, I wasn't expecting it to be that busy. There were no field trips or hockey games scheduled, so it would be a slow day. Which gave me time to update the drink board for the next week or two. This was one of my favorite parts of owning Hot Cider's. Coming up with drinks and the names. I usually picked names from books that I'd read lately.

A second popular drink that I kept on the menu, besides my cider, was a drink that I called Jax's Nips. It was a play on buttery nipples but with added Kahula and ice cubes and served with a blue shark straw. I made that available today, along with a new drink I'd come up with last night after finishing my latest book.

This one was a twist on a Hanky Panky with a spicy chili sugar rim that I named a Slippery Sloane. I'd had Billy taste it last night and I'd gotten the seal of approval. I'd just finished drawing a little fox in the corner of the board when my first customer came in.

As the hours went by, I had a steady amount of customers who came in after either shopping around the rink or having skated. There were a few kids who had obviously skipped school, but I wasn't going to narc. I'd had plenty of adventures myself when I was their age.

The Zamboni had been out once during the middle of the day. I liked to watch it move slowly around. The driver, Jack, was a mystery. He didn't socialize much. The only time I'd see him was when he was driving the Zamboni or spelling the ice when the rink closed and no humans were about. He was a thirst trap just waiting to be peeled open. His ancestry was hard to tell from the distance.

Soon enough, it was closing time. I'd accomplished everything on my to do list for the day and it had been steady. Profit and being organized for the win!

My fox snickered at me. I was only organized at the store. Everywhere else, I was like a hurricane blew in. It drove Billy absolutely nuts. I'd never met a goat that was as OCD as he was. If I purposefully left my dirty clothes around the apartment to mess with him, well, that's a best friend's job, right?

Closing time for the rink and some other shops was right around the corner. I locked the door about thirty minutes prior as I headed over to the rental skate's booth. I had just a little bit of time to play. My fox's tail started to move, almost vibrating, and I couldn't help the chuckle that slipped out.

Snow fell gently around the area. I tilted my chin up, enjoying the cool breeze. It never got too cold, thanks to one of the many spells around the rink, but it did snow continuously. It was literally a winter wonderland. It would be interesting to see it during the summer.

I handed over the cash for the rental skates. Quilo looked ready to sleep as he gave me a pair of skates. I held them up in front of me curiously. There was a splash of neon green paint on the right side of the right shoe, near the blade. The left shoelace was ripped. I looked at Quilo to ask for another, less broken, pair but he'd already left.

The skates might be well worn, but they fit like a glove. Some folks didn't think a big girl could balance enough to actually skate, but my fox helped with that. As I got onto the ice, thought paused and my senses took over. The blades slid easily as I moved along the side of the rink.

I'd started moving faster, my hair coming out of its bun. I'd just done one pass when I noticed Eirlys with a tall man by the wall. It looked like they were arguing. I'd usually just ignore her, but I felt like I owed her for the kindness she'd shown me the other night. Plus, I needed to try for Quinten.

Stupid feelings.

I stopped in front of them, holding onto the wall. "Uh, hi." I cleared my throat.

Eirlys turned to look at me. As did the man.

My fox and I stopped breathing. Mate. The man was my mate. Our bond flashed into existence and I lost my footing.

My ass hit the ice with a slap. Even with the extra cushion I carried, that was going to bruise. Ow. My fox even winced. That was a spectacular mess.

"Cider, are you okay?" Eirlys leaned over the wall in concern.

The man, my mate, jumped over the wall, his feet touching the ice gracefully, not even slipping. He knelt next to me, a concerned look in his eyes.

His eyes were a deep blue, almost teal color. His sunken cheeks were sharp and he had a long nose. His hair was black with silver at his temples.

Well, hello, silver fox.

"Bellissimo, my dear, are you hurt?"

I panicked. This beautiful portrait of a man was my mate and he was in front of me.

My clothing went flying as I shifted. I ended up tangled in my bra for several embarrassing seconds as I yipped. When I managed to untangle myself, my mate reached over as if to pick me up.

Couldn't have that. Nope. Full on panic mode hit and I scampered across the ice, not gracefully, I might add, since I ended up sliding several different directions as I ran away, before clambering over the wall. I ran as if my tail was on fire all the way home.

How could my mate be a vampire?

CHAPTER 2

Running among the trees, avoiding the roads, I knew that having a mate was a blessing, but I hadn't been expecting it to happen any time soon, if at all.

A mating bond wasn't something that could just be ignored. My fox had been shocked, but now, I was having to fight her for control. She wanted to go back to the silver haired stranger. He wasn't even a shifter. How could my mate be a vampire?

The house came into sight. I shook my fur out as I came to a stop at the front door. Billy was home. My nose twitched. He was making his vegetarian chili which was one of my favorites, even if it didn't have meat in it.

My shift was quick and I went inside quickly. I didn't feel like flashing the whole neighborhood my goodies.

"Hey," Billy yelled from the kitchen as I raced to my room. "Dinner is almost ready."

"Thanks." My voice trembled with the adrenaline that still coursed through me, my fingers shook. "Give me a few minutes." I yanked on sweatpants and a hoodie that I'd borrowed from Billy last year and never gave back. With it on, I started feeling more calm.

Billy and I had been best friends since elementary school. I know. A fox and goat. We were opposites in every way.

He was a vegetarian. I loved meat like I loved sweets. He was built like a mountain man axe thrower (It annoyed him when I said that. So, of course, I had to continue calling him that). He worked out, and it showed in the muscles in his arms and back. I, on the other hand, worked on binging my favorite shows and making sure my plumpness stayed that way. He was the sweetest mountain of a man and I, usually, was a total pain in the ass.

But we both supported each other through thick and thin. I helped out with his books for his landscaping business, Mountain Goats Landscaping, Llc.

His company was actually a hit around here because he used other goat shifters to keep his company 'green'. Need a field cut down? Flowers need to be trimmed? The goats have you covered. They even picked up after themselves when they left, if you get my meaning.

He helped me with my recipes. He cooked most nights, even though he worked just as much as I did.

His sister, Maya, liked to tease us that we were like an old married couple without the sexy time benefits. She wasn't wrong. It felt like that sometimes.

My best friend was a stud muffin. His girlfriends had a habit of saying he wrecked them. Most of them refused to leave his bed the first week.

"Hey, you okay?" Billy called, it sounded like he was heading toward my room.

"Not really." I pulled the hood over my head. "I have a

mate." Silence greeted me. I kept my head down as I pulled my hair out from under the fabric. "Can you believe it?"

"What do you mean that you have a mate?" Billy's sock covered feet appeared in my view. "Cider?"

Sighing, I lifted my head. Our eyes met and the world collided. His brow was furrowed as his one blue and one brown eyes widened in shock.

Oh, hot cocoa and marshmallows!

A mate bond snapped. Another one. Between my best friend and I.

I go my whole life without a mate and now, it's just wham bam thank you, ma'am.

"What... how?" Billy cleared his throat. His hands cupped my cheeks, pushing the hood back. "How is this possible?"

My fox purred, chattering at his goat. She pressed against me, urging me closer to him.

That's when Billy pressed his lips to mine with no hesitation. My hands gripped his shirt as my knees weakened. His beard was rough against my cheeks as the kiss deepened. His tongue swept into my mouth as if he were starving and it was the only thing that would save him.

My skin felt like it was going to ignite as his hands moved from my cheeks to the back of my neck. His big hands engulfed it, making me shiver, as he squeezed.

His tongue and mine danced, setting off fireworks inside of my stomach when the oven timer rang loudly enough that it shocked us out of whatever this was.

Billy pushed back away from me abruptly. I stumbled backward. If it weren't for my fox's quick reaction time, I'd have taken another assfall within an hour of the first.

"What the hell, Billy?" I grabbed onto my bed post.

The mating bond was clear to see between us. It was bright and a warm color. Comforting.

"Cider." He started to pace. Billy pulled on his hair. "How can this be possible? Mates? We've known each other all our lives! Of course I love you, but how is this possible?"

The timer went off again. Billy turned abruptly, leaving me on my own as he muttered under his breath.

I sat on the bed. I touched my lips gently. That kiss had been life changing.

I had two mates. My best friend was my mate. I scrubbed a hand down my face. I loved him. Always had, but I haven't kidded myself into thinking that anything could ever happen between us. I was happy being friends.

But now, that had all changed. His reaction said it all. He didn't want this and I didn't want to force anything on him. Rejection stung deep within me, swirling through my blood and making tears pool in my eyes.

He may not want me, but as soon as that bond had settled into place, my entire being called out for him to be mine.

And there wasn't anything that I could do to stop it.

Even though my stomach rumbled, I turned around and crawled onto the bed, curled around my stuffed fox pillow, and closed my eyes.

CHAPTER 3

Beep. Beep. Beep.

My alarm jerked me from sleep. I turned it off, before I glanced at my phone. No texts.

It was silent in the house. No bustling noises from the kitchen, which was strange. Billy was usually doing something in there in the mornings.

Rubbing my face, I sat up. Oh man. I needed to talk to someone. First though, I needed to get dressed and head out to work.

When I stopped in the kitchen, my thermos of tea sat in the middle of the countertop with a note from Billy.

Cider, emergency at a client's house. I'll see you this evening. We need to talk.

That wasn't ominous at all. I crushed the note in my hand, balling it up before throwing it in the trash.

Leaving early for once, I started the walk to the rink. My fox was uncharacteristically quiet, her silence filling me as we went to work.

I looked down at my phone and sent a text off to Maya.

You talk to Billy today?

I didn't have to wait long for a reply.

Other than he's avoiding you?

I snorted. That hurt a little but wasn't surprising. *So, he didn't tell you that a mate bond happened between us?*

The phone rang.

"What do you mean you two are mates?" Maya's voice had a note of excitement in it.

I hopped over a crack in the sidewalk before moving toward the woods as a shortcut to the rink. "It's a little more complicated than that." I sighed. "Maya, yesterday was a whirlwind. I have two mates."

Three heartbeats.

"Well, shit." She gave a short laugh. "You lucky fox. I'm going to need the full story."

The rink was around the corner as I hiked up the hill. I wasn't puffing yet, but I was going to need to sit down once I got to the store.

"When I have the full story, I promise to give it to you. Just don't say anything to Billy yet."

"Why don't you come over in a few days for a session? I know the kids would love to see you. You could even bring your frenemy and brother for some bonding time."

Maya ran a yoga studio out of her house. But with a twist. All her kids were goat shifters too. She taught yoga with goats. The kids loved it and so did her clients.

What can I say? She and her brother used their shifting abilities to make money. It was impressive. The humans loved it.

"Actually, that's not a bad idea. I know Quinten won't be able to say no. He loves Nico and all the others. Text me the details when you want this and I'll have Igor watch the shop for me."

Igor was my part time worker. She still worked for Iris'

flower shop, but when we became friends, she'd been bored, so I'd offered her the part time gig. She was also a Venus Fly Trap. She used to have an illusion spell from Iris' mom, but thanks to a few experiments, her mom created a spell that allowed Igor to actually shift.

I'd have to call her later to set it up once Maya texted me the information. Then I would have to talk to Eirlys and my brother. That would be a fun conversation. Quinten was still a little peeved at me for the glitter catastrophe.

Not to mention that other vampire was probably there as well. My vampire mate.

I just couldn't stop thinking about that.

"Sure thing, foxy lady. I'll text you. Have a good day at work! Dang it, Asher, stop trying to head butt your brother!" Maya hung up.

A chuckle slipped out. Asher was an ornery little dude. He'd be a heartbreaker when he grew up.

My fox stirred, her tail brushed against me. She chittered. Well, whatever was bugging her was no longer an issue. At least until her stubborn butt decided it did again.

The rink was in the center of all the shops. The castle on the hill was up on the mountain and easily seen anywhere anyone went.

As I passed Bitchin' Baubles that was owned by Thora, I noticed a crowd around one of the empty spaces further out from the rest of the stores, a large truck was outside of it with a logo that had me cursing. They were building another shop outside of the ring of stores? It would mess up the aesthetic for sure, not to mention who was building it.

Darcorp was a nationally recognized restaurant. If they were setting up a store here, I was in trouble. So was everyone else. The people around the truck were unfamiliar. A short balding man with a stringy looking mustache was giving orders while looking at a clipboard.

My fox's hair stood up and she gave a low growl. That made two of us. I flipped the open sign on the door as I unlocked it. One issue at a time. There was only so much I could do at once.

The door to the shop opened and Gray strutted inside. Like her name, her hair was gray and long. She'd been hinting at me when she'd visit sometimes that I needed to come down to her tattoo place, Lady Blue Tattoo, and get one done. I was still trying to decide if I wanted one or not.

"Hey, Cider." Gray moved with easy grace around the tables to end up at the counter, sitting at one of the stools. "I heard a little fox was seen running off the rink last night. Was that you?" She shrugged out of her jacket, her wolf tattoo with blue eyes vivid in the light.

I cursed. "Really? It's already all over that I freaked out?" I pulled out my box of loose leaf tea for her to look through to choose. "You look like shit, by the way."

Flipping me off with her left hand, she pointed to the chamomile tea with her right. "That's good for a hangover, right?"

"It sure is. With some lemon juice and honey, you'll be right as rain in a little bit." I snickered as I started putting the drink together.

"Rumor is that you met Eirlys' dad last night and he scared you so bad for the prank war, you shifted and ran away."

Almost dropping the kettle that was already hot, I whirled around. "Her dad?"

Gray held her hands up. "It's true? Do I need to go kick her ass?"

I shook my head, quickly finishing her tea, and handed

it to her. "No, he wasn't mean to me. I barely even said two words. It's just, er, he, um." How was I going to admit this?

"He? Stop stuttering." She blew on the hot beverage before taking a sip with a sigh. "Oh, that's good."

"He's my mate." My hands went flat on top of the counter as I looked down. He was her dad? Oh, that is so going to make this even more awkward than it already was.

"Your mate?" Gray blinked as she sipped more of her tea. "Well, that sucks."

"Tell me about it." If I could bang my head on the counter without risking damaging it, I would.

Once Gray left, I went through the scene from yesterday in my head. Every time I remembered shifting like a child, I groaned. How embarrassing. What must my new mate think of me?

A few customers came in, interrupting my inner battle. Right after them, Candela, the owner of Candela's Cupcake Shop walked in with her husky, who was always at her side, Jasper.

Looked like my shop was popular today.

She waited while I served the others in front of her.

"Hey, Candela. How are you? How's it going?" I offered a grin. "I am in love with those vanilla cupcakes with lavender frosting you did the other day."

"A little stressed. I'm sure you saw that building going up and who it belongs to?" Candela reached down, most likely unconsciously, and rubbed Jasper's ears. "I'm glad you like the cupcakes!"

Leaning over the counter, I tossed a puppy treat to Jasper. I kept the treats near the cash register. He caught it in mid air and happily munched it.

"Yeah, on my way in this morning. It gives me the

heebee jeebees." I poured a quick iced tea for her in a to-go cup.

"I'm wondering if we have the option to ask the rink owner not to let them in?" I rubbed the back of my neck. "It'd be great if we actually knew who the owner was.

She sipped her drink before shrugging. "It can't hurt to try to find out. Otherwise, we're all going to have to band together." She tried to hand me some cash, but I shook my head. "Thank you for the drink. I've got to go." She paused. "Oh, I almost forgot one of the reasons I wanted to see you. You know Jack?"

"The guy who drives the zamboni?" I knew the Jack she was talking about, but I didn't want to give away that I oogled him.

Candela grinned. "He mentioned earlier that he needed to talk to you. Something about skates and clothes on the ice?"

I groaned. I forgot about that. My clothes. The rented skates. Now, the zamboni driver had my clothes.

"I see that's a story you'll have to share later." Candela laughed as she left. "Good luck!"

I thumped my head on the counter.

The rest of the day was just as busy. Wednesday's usually included field trips from the schools in the afternoon skate time. Kids were everywhere. They usually had pocket money from their parents and loved the sweet drinks and popcorn.

It also was the worst day for clean up. That's why I didn't see him at first. I was busy scrubbing a table where a kid had left their chewed gum.

"Care for an extra hand?" His voice was deep and from behind me.

My body froze where I was leaning over the table. My

fox's hair moved as she puffed up her chest. I straightened slowly before turning.

He stood right in front of me. There was barely any room between us. His teal eyes darkened as our gazes collided. He was tall, almost as tall as Billy. He wasn't nearly as muscular, but his body made my mouth water as I moved my eyes down and back up briefly.

His grin was crooked, one of his fangs flashed against the light.

"Hello, Cider. I'm Titus, your mate."

CHAPTER 4

Titus leaned against the counter as I prepared him a drink. My fingers tingled from where I'd touched his chest to push him back from being so close. Why did I want him further away?

"So, are you not able to talk? I'm pretty sure my daughter said you talk a mile a minute if given an option." His voice was intoxicating, that deep accent had to be illegal in some parts of the country. I wanted to close my eyes and just listen.

But, I couldn't do that. I finished pouring the drink and turned with a saucy smirk.

"Your daughter?" I placed the drink in front of him. "Enjoy the Slippery Sloane."

It wasn't for the faint of heart.

"That's a different name." He raised his right eyebrow up elegantly as he took a sip. "Mmm. That's got a kick to it."

"I like to make drinks after book characters." My eyes watched his tongue flick out to taste the chili sugar. "I thought vampires couldn't eat normal food."

His grin almost made my legs weaken. "My dear, I am

an old vampire with refined tastes." He winked. "You like to read?" Good change of subject.

I found myself leaning against the counter, closer to him. "I love to read. The walls in my room are covered in books. My tablet is almost full with ebooks." I was getting excited like I usually did when it came to talking about it.

"Yeah? What are some of your favorites?" Titus took another sip of his drink.

"What genre are we talking about?" I laughed just as the shop's door opened with more customers. "Enjoy your drink, Titus." His name on my lips felt right and distracted me momentarily from the new customers.

An older woman who tended to come in often with her grandkids came up to the counter. The kids loved my virgin Hot Cider Original with popcorn. The grandmother sipped on a Jax's Nips as I talked with her, carefully avoiding the hot vampire whose eyes I could feel on me the entire time.

"Oh, these nips are delicious." The grandmother smacked her lips together as she moved to a table with me. "Almost as delicious as your fellow over there."

I sat in the chair across from her, coughing. "What? My fellow?" I glanced back over to Titus, who tipped his glass at me with a smirk. He'd heard that.

"It's obvious, deary. I'm old, not blind." She looked at her grandkids. "You're doing a great job with this place. Are you online? I can get the kiddos to write a review. If you keep the hottie around, I'm sure we can get thirsty ladies in." She wiggled her brows at me.

Titus choked, coughing as he thumped his chest behind me. I grinned.

"Yeah. I have a website and I'm on the review sites." I handed her one of my business cards that I usually had in one of my pockets at all times. "Thanks for the support!"

She and the kids headed out to the rink twenty minutes later. I hadn't stopped smiling since Titus had come into the shop.

"If you're going to just stand around, vamp, you could make yourself useful and help me clean some dishes." My hips swayed as I walked past him and through the small curtain to the back.

His shadow over my shoulder made me shiver. My fox wanted me to show him my neck.

"Anything that you ask for, I shall endeavour to provide." His breath brushed my ear lobe.

I couldn't help it. I pushed my ass against him as I stopped walking. His growl echoed through the small back room and his hands dug into my hips. I turned to look up at him as my hands ran up his shirt.

"You know this can never work." My voice hitched as he bent, his lips touching the top of my ear again.

"Why do you say that?" His tongue flicked out, caressing the sensitive skin, and I gasped.

"I'm a shifter. Not to mention, you're Eirlys' dad." My protest was weak as his hands moved down to grip my asscheeks.

"I don't see a reason yet." His lips finally moved. He kissed me like he was starving.

I tasted orange from the drink. His tongue thrust into my mouth. My fingers dug into his shirt. More. I needed more. Everything short circuited.

He shifted, pulling me up, my legs instantly wrapped around his legs as he set me on the side of the sink. I had to pull back to gasp for air as his lips moved down my throat. His fangs brushed my skin as goosebumps ran down my arms.

Holy puffy sugar cones. This guy was strong.

There was a sound from the front when suddenly Eirlys came into the back room as we pulled back from each other. I felt like a teenager caught while Titus just looked slightly annoyed.

"Cider, I have got to tell you what just happened, you are never going to--" She pulled to a stop and her eyes went wide. "Freaking A, Titus! What the hell is wrong with you?" She planted her hands on her hips. "That is not how you romance your newly found mate. We talked about this for shit's sake!"

My mouth popped open in shock. They'd talked about us? About romancing me?

Titus gently thumped his forehead on my shoulder. "Lys, my dear, why are you ruining my moment?"

"Groping Cider in the back of her store when anyone could come in? What are you? One hundred?" Her foot started to tap.

A giggle slipped out. My frenemy was cock blocking her father.

"Contrary to your opinion, Lys, I know how to romance my own mate." Titus straightened as his hands moved down my back. "Would you mind giving us some privacy?"

"Did you not listen to a word that I just said?" Eirlys bent suddenly, taking off her right heel and threw it with precision.

It smacked Titus right in the face before it flopped to the ground.

I lost it. My chest jiggled as I clutched my sides. Titus rubbed his forehead where a red spot had occurred with the imprint of it. He looked at me, his eyes softening.

"Cider, I'll stop by later so that we can talk." He took my right hand and kissed the top of it. "Behave, Eirlys." He glared at her as he walked out.

Eirlys shook her head at him before turning back to me.

"So, I know we aren't exactly friends, but I thought you needed to see this." She held a tablet in her well manicured hands. "Darcorp is already starting to try to push us out. I know you talked to Candela. I think we need to discuss this before this jackass tries to ruin everyone's stores." She handed the tablet to me.

A picture of a flyer was on the screen advertising the grand opening soon. They were offering free skate rentals for the first two months with a meal purchase from their attached restaurant.

"They'll lose any profit with this." My fox was growling. "It'll bring customers to them and away from the rest of us who serve food and drinks." I handed the tablet back. "We've barely just opened. If a big corporation pulls this stunt, I know I won't survive the loss of profit enough to pay rent and supplies." I started to pace.

"We have some issues." Eirlys crossed her arms, her fingers tapping on her arms. "Cider, I may have overreacted about the cups. I think we both escalated a silly issue. But we did some pretty great pranks. With that kind of ingenuity, why don't we join forces against the greater evil?"

Eirlys was a straight shooter. It was one thing I grudgingly respected. Plus, she was family now. I paused. Oh God.

"Okay, but I need to ask this." I had a hard time not grinning, my lips twitched. "If you're my brother's mate BUT I'm also your father's mate, am I your sister-in-law or your step-mom now?"

CHAPTER 5

The plan began to take shape. The first thing we'd decided on was that we needed to fight intelligently. There was no way we could afford free gifts for two months for each customer. But we could show the community we supported them.

Eirlys already had that started since she sponsored the hockey team. She would work on a few things with them.

I needed to figure out what to do for my part. I was going to talk to Billy for ideas. Once he stopped avoiding me. He hadn't responded to any of my texts today. We needed to still talk about what happened between us and now what happened with Titus.

I figured I could try to offer an olive branch between us, until we figured out this mate thing, by bringing home one of his favorite sandwiches from Bob's Diner. It would give me a chance to get a big fat rare burger with all the mushrooms piled on top of it.

I was practically salivating as I thought about the burger as I locked up. A shudder ran up my spine and my fox's hearing detected someone behind me.

When I turned, my fingers curled as my nails lengthened. The balding man who had been bossing around the crowd of people was behind me with a nasty glint in his eyes. I hid my hands behind my back. He was human, so I needed to watch my shifting around him.

"Can I help you?" Billy would be proud. I didn't hiss at him. My fox was ready to rip this guy to shreds and it wasn't because he worked for Darcorp.

The guy looked me up and down before answering. "Yes, I'm Samuel and I'm the manager of the Darcorp store opening up down the way. I'm going around to each of the new neighbors to introduce myself. I've heard of your special cider drink that's a rage around the area. Very impressive."

He didn't look impressed. On the contrary, as he pressed his lips in a tight line, he looked constipated and annoyed.

"Thanks?" I moved sideways. "Nice to meet you." Not really. "Welcome to the rink. I've got to head out."

Samuel just nodded and gave a wave. "I'm sure we'll see more of each other."

I sped up my walk to get to my car. That hadn't been weird or creepy at all. My skin crawled as if bugs were running along it.

My car was right where I'd left it yesterday with a small covering of snow. As I got into it, I sent a text to Billy about picking up dinner. I didn't get a response back right away, but I knew what he liked.

Yet, when I got home, Billy wasn't home. He wasn't responding to my texts or phone calls.

I called Maya.

"Where is your pig headed brother?" I was trying not to get mad but failed miserably at it.

Maya snorted. "I told him to reply to you, but nnnooo. He had to be a man." Her voice rose. "Stop hiding in your nephews' room and go home to talk to your mate!" There was a scuffling sound. "I'll send him back to you in a little bit."

I snapped. "No. It's fine. Tell him not to come home tonight or I'll bite his balls off for being a pansy ass." I hung up. If I was in my fox form, my hair would be standing up.

Was it really that bad of a thing that I was his mate? Sure, I wasn't a skinny girl, but I tried to be a good person. Granted, I was kind of a hot mess. I had good fashion sense though, right? I mean, spikes on shirts were kickin'.

I put the food in the fridge as I fumed. I wouldn't be able to eat right now. That's when I remembered that my favorite bra was still with Jack at the rink.

It was the perfect excuse I needed. I threw my clothes off, leaving them on the ground in the living room knowing that it would annoy Billy when he returned home.

My paws clattered on the floor before I ran out of the house, snow flying around me. Unlike the last shift, I took the time to enjoy my run. My limbs were lithe and I was quiet as I ran toward the rink, jumping over branches and bushes. I felt free.

It was all too soon when the shops came into view. By the time I scurried along the foam sidewalks that were specifically designed so people could walk along them in their skates, most of the stores were shut down. I went looking for the small maintenance building where Jack usually was. He never really left the area. I think he actually slept there.

Luck was on my side because the door was opened. Looked like Jack was cleaning up in the small building.

My fox gave an excited chitter as we wound around

boxes on the ground. This would be the first time since opening Hot Cider's that we'd actually get to see the mysteriously grumpy zamboni driver up close.

There was noise in the back of the room that I followed. Jack was bending over a box, cursing about missing parts.

A streak of mischief ran through me. Before I could think better of it, I launched myself onto the box, next to his face.

Jack jerked a little, looking up with a scowl on his face. When he saw me, his scowl faded but then he jerked like he'd been burned as I almost fell off the box.

Mate.

Oh, come on!

Are you kidding me?

The universe had to be playing with me.

How could I be lucky enough to have three!? The bond was there though.

That's exactly what happened. Jack straightened, the frown back on his face.

Looking at him up close, I wanted to lick my lips. He was just scrumptious. Tall, but not as muscular as Billy, closer to Titus in shape. More on the slender side. His dark skin, the color of ebony, made my mouth water. Biting him would be fun.

"You must be Cider." He walked over to a table against the wall and picked up a bundle of clothes. "These are yours. Try not to shift on the ice again, would you?" He placed them next to me as he continued to talk. It was like he didn't even notice that a bond had formed. I was still staring in shock. "It shouldn't be my job to return these to you."

Maya was going to have a field day. I huffed, grabbed

the clothes in my mouth and jumped behind a tall pile of boxes.

"So, are you just going to ignore that we're mates?" I'd shifted and started pulling on the clothes.

"I don't even know you. I can't be mates with someone I don't know." His tone was snide and I wanted to throw something at him. Thoughts of biting him for pleasure turned to biting for another reason.

"You're not human. You know that mate bonds don't work like that. Mates are mates." I buttoned up my jeans and walked out from behind the boxes with my hands on my hips.

Two mates that didn't want me and one that did.

He looked up at me from whatever he was doing.

Holy guacamole.

I finally got a straight look at his features.

His face was striking, cheeks sunken in with a sharp square jaw. His hair was cropped short and a shade darker than his ebony skin. His eyes. Oh man. He had some Asian ancestry in him somewhere with his almond shaped eyes.

My fox rolled over to give her belly to him. I had to fight not to actually do it.

His eyes were clear, just blue enough for color, but light enough that it felt like I was falling into a frozen pond. He most certainly was not human.

"That might be how the bond works, but it doesn't mean I have to accept it. I don't know you, and honestly?" His striking features sneered as he glanced up and down. "You're not exactly my type, sweetheart."

It felt like my heart shattered. The blood left my face.

"Excuse me?" I tried to clear my throat. "I'm not your type?"

"Look," he shifted his shoulders, "I'm Jack Frost. The

Winter King. Heart of ice? I'm not interested in having a mate." His voice had hardened, cooled. "You have another mate, if I'm not mistaken. Go chase him."

Just like that, I was dismissed as he turned his back on me.

I was too hurt to come up with anything to say so I left. I felt numb. Again.

Not only did my best friend reject me, another mate, who I didn't know and who didn't know me, just told me to stuff it basically. That I wasn't his 'type'.

If having multiple mates was going to hurt this much, I wasn't sure I wanted them either.

CHAPTER 6

The house was dark as I walked in. I sniffed a little as I headed to the fridge. It was definitely time for some food, wine, and chocolate.

With my arms full, I closed the door with my hip. I hadn't turned on the light, I could see just fine as I made my way to my room.

"Cider?" Billy's concerned tone came from his room.

I hadn't heard him because I'd been too focused on the food in my arms. My heart still ached from the rejection from earlier, I wasn't sure I wanted to deal with Billy being an idiot.

"What?" Standing in front of my door, I tried to figure out how I was going to open it. Maybe I could try to balance on one foot and use the other to open the door knob.

"Cid, I'm sorry for pulling away." His heat was against my back. "That was childish and if it hurt you, I'm sorry." His hands touched my arms.

Just like that, my body melted, leaning into his chest and it irritated me. Billy was my best friend first and foremost. His reaction wasn't surprising, he was bad with change.

I tilted my head back, looking up into his multi colored eyes. "It did hurt. I can't just turn this off. Neither can you or the other two, no matter how much any of us may want to."

"Two?" His brows rose high. "There's another one?"

"Surprise." If my response was a little dry, you couldn't blame a girl. "Do me a favor and open the door, would ya?"

He leaned over my shoulder to pop open the door and I pushed it with my hip.

"Look. Today really sucked. I'm going to drown myself in comfort food and alcohol. You can join if you want." I dropped the food and placed the wine on my desk before brushing my hands together before looking at him.

The big lumberjack looked exhausted. I noticed the circles under his eyes now that I paid attention. His clothes looked rumbled. Even his beard looked messy. He groomed that with vanity and pride. Usually, he took longer than a teenage girl to care for it in the mornings.

I'd been so focused on how I felt, I hadn't even thought about how this would affect him. Not very best friend-like of me.

"Hey, goat face." My arms wound around his waist as I gave him a hug. "I'm sorry I was a brat. This is a crazy and scary development. I'm here and ready to talk when you're ready. We'll figure this out together, just as we always do."

Billy held my face between his hands. "I hurt you." The tortured expression cut me deep. "I never meant to do that. You're my best friend. I love you, Cider."

My broken heart skipped a beat, warming slightly.

"I love you, too." I touched his chest, moving my hands

to rest over his heart. "I'm scared that I fucked up our relationship."

Billy snorted, his eyes lighting up in amusement. "Cider, you are a lot of things. But a fuck up? It's not one of them." He moved his face closer to mine as I tipped my chin up. "This is just a new step in our lives. It explains why I never settled down. Something always felt off with other women. You're the only one I've ever been able to actually be myself with." The corners of his eyes crinkled. "You're the only woman who's not afraid to call me out on my shit and try to kick my ass at video games."

"Billy, I hate to tell you this." I closed my eyes, trusting him. "You suck at video games."

His scoff was cut off as he pressed our lips together. The scruff of his beard was a new sensation against my face, but it wasn't unpleasant.

When his tongue swept into my mouth, twining with mine, I moaned. It was like sweet honey with fresh pine. My fox was thrilled. She trilled her excitement, making my chest hum.

Pulling back from him for a second, I pushed his chest slightly as I moved to pull his shirt over his head. He shucked it over his head before pushing his pants off.

My mouth dried as I looked at my best friend naked. I'd seen him pretty close to it. Billy liked his shorts and nothing else usually. But naked is a whole other ballgame.

I barked out a laugh.

"A tattoo?" He had a small goat standing on a hill on his right inner thigh, right next to his cock. "How did I not know you had a tattoo?" It was actually pretty cute.

Billy cleared his throat. "My ex did it. Remember, she was apprenticing as a tattoo artist? I was drunk one night. Woke up with it."

I trailed a finger along the goat's small horns. Billy shivered. "I like it."

Suddenly, I was in the air and bouncing onto the bed. Billy had tossed me onto it easily. Damn, that was hot.

"Glad you like it. I'd like you to pay attention to my cock now, if you could." His grumble filled the room, shooting straight to my pussy.

My clothes were off in record time as I sat up on my knees. I didn't even hesitate to worry if he wouldn't like my stretch marks. This was Billy. My big, kind, overbearing lumberjack.

By the way he was devouring me with his gaze, I'd have to say he liked what he saw.

I knew a second later just how much when I was on my back staring up at him. His expression was soft as he bent to brush our lips together.

"You're perfect. I love how you own every inch of your skin." His hands rested on either side of my face as he held himself over me. "You're mine now."

"Ye--S!!" My answer ended on a loud croak as he impaled my pussy with his cock. I shuddered as pleasure coursed through me. "Oh, fuck!"

Billy shifted his weight to his hand, gripping my right leg and put it up over his shoulder, gripping my knee. The shift in position allowed him to thrust in deeper and I could only just hang on for the ride.

I gripped his wrist with one hand, while with my free one, I moved to start rubbing my clit in circles in time with his thrusts. I could barely keep up.

Pleasure flooded my senses. I could barely breathe properly. It was unlike anything I'd experienced before. This was right. This was everything. My body was his and his was mine.

"Cider!" he groaned my name as he reached his climax. His hips moved rapidly and I followed shortly after, leaving me a panting hot mess.

Holy shit.

CHAPTER 7

"Here." Billy handed me a bowl of chocolate ice cream. "It's the perfect breakfast after being up all night."

"Thanks." I had a hard time concentrating on anything besides watching him walk around in just boxers. "You're the one who kept us up all night."

I'd seen him like this before, and I'd appreciated the eye candy, but now that it was mine? I just couldn't seem to stop watching him.

"My eyes are up here." He sat next to me with his own bowl, his teeth flashed in amusement as he scooped up a large bite of his ice cream.

"Such pretty eyes, too." I batted my eyelashes at him as he laughed.

"We still need to talk." He leaned against the head-board, his feet relaxed on the bed as he took another spoon of the cool treat.

I had my own mouthful before replying. "Honestly, I've loved you as my best friend for how long? Being my mate just brings us closer and I'm excited for it. Now, I know you're not thrilled, but..."

Billy put the back of his spoon on my lips to silence me. "You've still got a bad habit of talking and not listening." He raised his right brow.

I shrugged but motioned for him to continue.

"I freaked out. That's on me. But it wasn't because we're mates. It's because I never thought I'd have one. I'm thirty-five. Most goats find their mates in their early twenties. So when it snapped into existence, I freaked out."

He set the bowl on my nightstand.

"I'm thrilled that my mate is my best friend. Am I happy that you have two more? No, but I'll learn to deal." His fingers ran down my cheek. "I love you and that love is going to evolve and I can't wait for it." His head bent and our lips met for a brief, tender kiss.

"You suck." My face was on fire as I turned away from him to finish my ice cream.

"No, pretty sure you're the one doing the sucking."

I coughed, choking on the spoonful of frozen goodness until Billy banged on my back a few times.

"You're an ass." I wiped my mouth with the back of my hand as I narrowed my eyes at him.

His lips twisted but he didn't say anything other than to look smug. I shook my head, grabbed our empty bowls, dropped them off in the sink, and came back to curl against his chest.

His big arms pulled me close and kissed my forehead. "We will figure this out. It may just take time. In the meantime, I'm not going anywhere."

As I lay with him, enjoying the delightful warmth, my phone chimed. Billy handed it to me. It was a text from my brother.

Hey. You free for a run?

I blinked. It was the first time he'd voluntarily reached

out to me in weeks. Billy noticed who it was when he'd given me my phone and squeezed my shoulders.

"Go for it. You need to talk to him." His hands were warm.

Sure. See you at the spot in five minutes.

I sat up, pulling away from my mates chest.

"I'll be back in a bit. We need to talk about the other two in the picture." Placing my phone on the dresser, I opened my window that faced out to the woods. I shifted and with a hop, I was running to a small clearing that Quinten and I used growing up to have sibling meetings away from mom or dad.

I let my fox take over. She knew where we were going. I needed to think.

Quinten had been so mad at me when I'd tricked Eirlys into drinking the potion I'd purchased from The Magical Rooster. Not because it had ended up making Eirlys have explosive glitter orgasms for a few days, or that it turned his dick blue, but because it had made Eirlys cry.

He refused to talk to me until I apologized. Even after that, he'd been avoiding me. Hopefully, today would be a way to give an olive branch to him and Eirlys. I was going to ask them to yoga with Maya.

Quinten was already there. He had a backpack next to him where he sat on a log. His eyes tracked me as I moved to sit in front of him. I sat and wagged my tail once.

"Hey." Quinten patted my head like he usually did to annoy me. "Here's a robe for you." He pulled out the robe from the pack and tossed it on top of me. "Just yell when you're dressed." He turned his back to give me a sense of modesty that wasn't needed.

The robe was soft. My feet were freezing but I grabbed the pack he'd left and used it to stand on.

"Okay. We're good."

Quinten turned around. He snorted loudly when he noticed I was standing on the back pack but he didn't say anything.

"Thanks for coming, sis." He sat down again. "Sit with me."

"So." I awkwardly plucked at the robes belt. "How much longer are you going to hate me? I was just so mad about the ch--" I choked on the word.

Quinten was quiet for several long moments.

"Eirlys is my mate, Cider. She means everything to me. I shouldn't have told her about the chickens. I didn't know that she and Jace would use that on you." His hands rested on his knees. "She said you were working together now."

Nodding, my shoulders slumped a little. "I may have gone overboard before, but she's shown that she's a good person. I was actually going to invite her to yoga. Why don't you all come?"

Quinten bumped our shoulders together. "I love you, squirt. We'll be there tomorrow morning."

"Good. Maya and the kids will be happy to see you." I rubbed my arm awkwardly. "Are we going to be okay, Quint? I miss you."

My brother was silent for a few moments before he wrapped an arm around my shoulder, squeezing it. "We'll be okay. It just might take a little time."

We shared a smile before I shifted again and ran back home.

CHAPTER 8

When I got home, Billy was making eggs and Maya was sitting across from him at the island.

"So, you two got over your issues?" Maya brushed her purple hair off her shoulder. She sipped a cup of tea.

"Don't ask questions you don't want the answers to, sis." Billy moved the eggs from the frying pan to a plate.

She rolled her eyes at him as she turned to me as I sat next to her.

"Have you checked your reviews on the website?" Her brows were furrowed as she glanced at her phone. "Or the other shops?"

"No. Not lately. Why?" I took her phone. "A regular mentioned it the other day that she was going to leave one."

"I was going through the website to buy some tickets to one of the hockey games, and I noticed the stars on most of the shops went down, but especially yours." She pointed to my shop's little page.

Two stars. The hot cider was mediocre at best.

Two stars. It was meh.

One star. The place was dirty.

There were about ten more negative reviews that were posted last night. Before that, most of the reviews had been positive and glowing.

"How is this possible? My place is never dirty! The only place that's dirty is my room!"

Maya took her phone back as I stood and kicked the stools legs.

"The other shops have basically the same reviews, just small changes." Maya pondered.

I paused. Darcorp. That sleazy yuck face arsehat. He'd been strange yesterday.

"It's that cockroach Samuel. Who else would have any reason to do this?" My fingers ran through my hair. "Ugh!" My foot kicked the bar stool leg again and I jumped up and down. "Ow!"

Billy turned off the stove, moved around the island, and picked me up. It was like I was a pillow. That was hot. He put me on the island next to Maya, who rolled her eyes at me.

"Let's see." Billy shook his head as he bent to look at my foot. His touch was comforting. "It'll be alright in a few minutes." His hand ran up my thigh, making me shiver.

"Okay, do that later, you two." Maya reached up and slapped Billy in the back of the head. "Are we all set for yoga tomorrow?"

"Oh! Right!" I smiled happily. "Yes, and Quinten is going to come with Eirlys and her other mates."

"Well, that'll make the kids happy." Maya sipped her tea. "So, you going to tell me about your other mates?"

Billy froze for a second before he blew out a breath.

"I need to meet them, too." He brushed a kiss on my forehead. "Invite them to dinner tomorrow."

"Holy shite. Did my brother just do something mature?" Maya blinked as I snorted.

"Why are you here again?" Billy glared at his sister. "Shoo. Go away."

They started bickering good naturedly. I left them to it. I needed to talk to Eirlys and see if she had any ideas about what to do about the reviews.

I also needed to get Titus' information. Not to mention, I needed to talk to Jack Frigging Frost. I was going to give him a piece of my mind for what he said.

Thinking about my other two mates made me blush. Especially thinking about that make out session with Titus. Oh my God. That man could kiss. His tongue was out of this world.

Jack, on the other hand, I just wanted to smack his head a few times with my paws. Possibly rip up his clean clothes and pee on them.

I was in front of Hot Cider's before I realized I'd driven on auto pilot here and gotten out of the car. There was a paper taped to the front door. It had a soft scent of lavender on it.

I had a few minutes to get ready before opening, so I opened it as soon as I unlocked the door.

It was from Titus. My heart rate kicked up.

My beautiful fox, I'll see you later this afternoon. We should talk.

Oh, yeah. Talking was a good idea. Maybe after there would be kissing. Because that was a very good motivator for me.

Just as the store opened, a customer stepped inside and I had to put away the letter. The day was busy. I wasn't sure why, but there was an influx of people skating and shopping today. I'd had a pleasant conversation with a new resident of Silver Springs.

She was a short thing, barely five feet. She was round, like me, and she had long auburn hair. Another redhead to add to our arsenal in the town! Her green eyes were distracting because her pupils were slightly elongated like a cats but she was human. It was possible that she had a relative in the past who was a shifter.

"Hi!" Her attitude was refreshing with how bouncy she was. "I'm Vida Simmone. This is my first time to the rink, but a nice old lady outside said this was the place to get a drink to warm up with."

"It certainly is the place for a good drink. Stiff or not." I gestured to the menu. "What are you in the mood for?"

She tapped her foot, as if she couldn't quite keep still. "I have to go to work in a few hours, so I should be good. Can I try the original?"

"Sure can." I rang up the drink and took her payment. "I'll have that ready in a minute."

Instead of going to one of the tables, she sat at the counter. "This place seems so magical. I love it so much."

"It really does, doesn't it?" If only she knew. "It's one of the many reasons I opened up my shop here."

"The only thing that kind of made me sad about this place is that I saw Darcorp was putting up a shop. This place just doesn't give off the kind of vibe to have that kind of place." Vida took the hot cider from me as I placed it in front of her. "Oh! This is so good!" She didn't even blow on it before gulping it down.

I liked that she didn't like seeing Darcorp. Hearing it from a customer was nice.

"Some of us aren't too pleased either, but we have great

customers like you, so we aren't too worried." That was a big lie.

After Vida left, I rolled my shoulders. There were no new customers, so I had a chance to call Triple E. Eirlys picked up on the second ring.

"Triple E. Eirlys speaking. How can I help you?" She sounded distracted.

"Hey, uh, it's Cider. I know we're going to see each other tomorrow morning, but I was wondering if you'd noticed the new reviews that popped up overnight?" I started to wipe down the counter.

"Hey. Yeah, actually, I saw them this morning. Think it's Darcorp?" She sounded weary.

"I think it's Samuel, at the very least. He's the manager, in case he didn't end up at your place yet to introduce himself. He was being all sleazy yesterday after closing. Most of those reviews are all the same except for the names of the shops. I was thinking we could contact the website host and see if they could do anything?" Some of the flavor bottles needed to be refilled and I bent under the counter to grab some new ones. "And I was thinking about getting back at him. He has such a super fancy car. I have a few things that could be done to mess with it." Placing the box of new bottles on the counter, I mumbled, "dear readers, please don't do any of these pranks for the author will not be responsible for damages."

I had several rolls of saran wrap that I hadn't used the past few months. That would be perfect. I grabbed a few of the rolls.

"What was that last part?" Eirlys spoke louder over someone in the background.

"Nothing! Just making a reminder for myself is all. So, what do you say? Take the battle to them?"

"Yes. He started it. Let's do it." I could hear the grin in her voice. "No one messes with the Silver Springs Ice Rink family. We will make more plans tomorrow."

We hung up. That's when I noticed the zamboni on the ice. Jack.

My fox bristled. I needed to talk to him. There had to be a reason he was being such a jerkwad.

As I flipped the sign on the door, letting any customers know that I'd be back in a few minutes, and walked out, Titus was there.

Tall, sexy, dangerous Titus. His blue eyes made my toes curl just by gazing at me.

"Hello, Cider." That deep voice.

"Hi." My voice was barely a whisper as he leaned into my space, his lips brushing mine.

"Where are you headed off to?" His fingers brushed along my cheeks.

"I was going to go yell at Jack for being a dick." But Titus was distracting me with his touch.

He paused, his hands resting on my shoulders. "Jack?"

"Yeah, so, looks like I have three mates now." I leaned into him, forgetting that I was holding rolls of saran wrap for a few brief moments. "Surprise?"

Titus threw back his head, letting out a large belly laugh. His chest heaved as he fought to calm down, but every time he looked down at me, looked to the rink, he started all over again.

I started to tap my foot. "Are you done? I don't know why it's so funny."

"No, dear one. I'm not laughing at you." Titus wiped at his eyes. "Jack is an old friend. I can only imagine what he said to you. He's a little bit of a grump."

I stopped my foot as he pulled me against him again.

"Oh. So, it's not because it's me?" That eased tension in me I hadn't been aware had been there.

"Baby girl." Titus' husky voice filled my ears. "There is absolutely nothing wrong with you. Jack has his own issues." His lips caressed my neck. "Why don't I talk with him?"

"You don't need—oh God." My voice squeaked as he bit down on my collarbone with soft pressure. "We're in public!" I hissed but didn't give much of a fight.

"Does that turn you on?" His hands moved to my backside, stroking my back.

"Surprisingly, yes." I shuddered. "But, I own a store here and I can't afford to get arrested."

"Mmm. You have a point." Titus gave a cocky tilt of his head. "I'll talk to Jack tonight. Then we can all talk together. Does that sound good?"

"Actually, yeah. Um, Billy wants to meet you, too. Maybe we can all have dinner?" I was suddenly feeling shy. "I have tomorrow off. Would that work?"

His fingers went back up to cup my cheeks. "I will see you tomorrow evening with the jerkwad." His amusement made my spine tingle. He gave me a lingering kiss before he walked off.

I ended up watching him until he was gone. I shook my head. Damn. I had something to do.

The parking lot was full, but as I moved around, sniffing the air for Samuel's scent, I made sure there wasn't anyone around when I finally found it.

His scent stunk. It permeated the air around the sleek luxury sedan. It was black. Which was perfect. I got to work.

No matter what someone thinks. It takes time to wrap a whole car with hundreds of feet of plastic film. I had to duck behind the car a few times when someone came into view. It took about thirty minutes to finish. I took a picture and scurried back to the store.

If the sun got too hot and melted the plastic to the paint? Well, that wasn't my fault that he took so long to get to his car.

CHAPTER 9

"Wait, wait." Igor held up her hands. "You suddenly just got three mates in two days?" She was laughing her ass off at me.

I rolled my eyes at my part time worker who helped out on the days I took off. She'd come in after closing to talk about next week's hours.

"Yes, three. But let's talk about you. How's it going with Lawrence now that he's able to shift into a human like you?"

She usually worked for FFS You Need Flowers!

She was hellbent on taking over the world and had decided she wanted experience with interacting with humans before making her plan.

She was a hard worker and hilarious.

"Lawrence is a prat. Like, he has a permanent stem up his ass. He hates that I'm not nice." She flipped her very curly black hair over her shoulder. "Let's not talk about that limp noodle."

I finished filling up the flavor bottles. Man, I was

running low on my secret ingredients to the original. I'd have to call to order some tomorrow after yoga.

"Alright, no limp noodle talk." I put away the bottles. "How's everyone else at home?"

"Oh dear Gods." Ever the dramatic, Igor posed with her hand on her forehead. "Those three men of Iris' are trying to see who can fuck the most. I can guarantee you that as soon as I left the shop, Iris and Dorian started to hump each other."

Snorting, I leaned against the counter.

"So everyone is good."

Igor shuddered visibly. "There's going to be little Irises around soon. I just know it."

"Well, if you ever want more hours to get away." I raised an eyebrow at her. "Business is picking up, so I could probably afford to pay you three days a week."

"I told you that you didn't need to pay me." Her scoff was loud and filled with annoyance. "Working here is good practice and gives me more data."

"I still have to pay you, Igor." That's when a thought hit me. "What would you do against someone plotting against you?"

I swear her eyes gleamed. I could just see the wheels turning in her mind.

"I can only assume you're talking about Darcorp? Gossip travels fast around here. I'm guessing you don't want anyone eaten?" She pursed her lips as I shook my head no. "Okay, just basic. I can work with it. How about messing with the plumbing? I can have a few friends burst the pipes when he's trying to get it installed."

I blinked. "Like those movies where someone is in a porta potty and it explodes?" That actually sounded like a lot of fun, as long as no one got hurt. But it seemed a little excessive at this point. I'd wait until I'd gotten to speak with Eirlys tomorrow morning before making any decisions.

"Exactly like that. Let me know if you want help doing it." She tilted her head to the side. "It's time for me to get back home. Iris is hopeless without my help in the greenhouse. Later." She swaggered out the door, her curly hair flouncing everywhere.

I finished up closing and headed back home. It was going to be an interesting next few days. That was for sure.

CHAPTER 10

"Welcome!" Maya had her walk out basement french doors wide open. "Come in, come in." Her monkey eating a Pop-Tart printed leggings were bright neon. I had to blink a few times.

"Why are you a morning person?" I chugged down my black tea.

"The early worm gets the bird." Her cheerful tone grated on my ears.

"Wait. That's not the saying." I set my thermos on a table near the door. "Where are the kids?"

"They're finishing their breakfast before coming down." Maya handed me a mat. "Set up wherever you'd like."

"Maya!" Quinten came through the doors with his arms spread. "You look great!"

Maya hugged him, laughing. "Quinty! Look at how tall you've gotten."

He snorted. "You just saw me last week." He turned as Eirlys walked inside with a mat under her arm. "This is Eirlys."

"Oh my. Your aura is gorgeous!" Maya pulled her into

her arms, smushing Eirlys in her boobs. "Welcome to Goat Salutation Yoga Studio!"

I snickered softly as Quinten went to separate Maya from his mate.

"Aunt Cid!" a soft female voice called out.

Riley, the only girl of the kids, came running into the room. I swept her up into my arms.

"Hey, little fish." Her nickname came when I'd caught her talking to her goldfish a few years ago. "You ready to kick your brothers' butts in today's session?"

"You know it." She grinned, one of her front teeth was missing.

"Good." I set her down. "Go shift, little fish."

She ran back up the stairs yelling for her brother, Eli.

"Alright." Maya clapped her hands together. "Let's get everyone set up before the rest of the class arrives."

I was setting up my mat next to Eirlys when a shiver went down my spine. I glanced over my shoulder and smiled as Titus walked in. He was wearing loose grey sweatpants that made my mouth water. His shirt clung to him as he walked over to us.

"Hello, my fox." He pressed a kiss to my lips gently. "Hello, little snowdrop." He looked at Eirlys gently before narrowing his eyes at Quinten and her two other mates that had come with. "*Rattos.*"

I choked on my laugh as Eirlys smacked his arm. "Titus! Be nice!"

He scoffed before setting up his place next to me as more supes started filing through the door for the class. Maya had two sessions a day. The morning was for supernaturals while the afternoon was for humans or supes.

"Namaste, my beautiful beauties." Maya stood in front of the class, starting her spiel. I glanced at Titus in the corner of my eye, he winked at me cheekily and I smiled.

"Let's start with mountain pose." Maya put her hands above her head as the class began copying her movements. "This is a time of reflection. Focus on your breathing. The goats will be down momentarily."

My muscles warmed as we moved through the poses. By the time we had gotten into plank, the clatter of hooves came rushing into the room.

Four baby goats of various colors started sniffing at the clients. Riley, a light brown with spots, came to butt gently against my forehead with her head. Her tiny tail wagging crazily.

Another goat, about twice her size, ran in front of the class, and jumped on his mother's back. Maya didn't even bat an eye as she transitioned to the next pose.

"Yes, yes, Cole. You're the king of the studio. We get it." Maya moved into downward dog pose, making Cole jump from her.

The youngest of the four, Nico, dashed right up to Titus' face and screamed. Titus just snorted, acted like he fell over and cowered in fear.

It was actually pretty cute. I was grinning when I noticed Eirlys watching me with a smile of her own.

"What?" My face red, I turned back to watch Maya.

"Nothing. It's just, I don't think I've ever seen you actually look happy like that. It's a little weird that my father does that, but I'm no one to judge." She looked over her shoulder at her mates who were playing with Asher and Riley, completely ignoring the yoga part.

"So," she brought her focus back. "What are we going to do about Darcorp and Samuel? The reviews were bad enough, but now I'm hearing rumors of suppliers running out of merchandise because someone bought everything up."

That was news to me. Maybe pranks weren't the answer for this.

We moved into warrior pose. The kids started running through the tunnels that everyone's legs made. Asher in the lead of the small race.

"How do we know if it was Samuel?" My brow furrowed.

Eirlys shrugged. "We don't, but it's an awfully big coincidence."

We moved to clasp our hands in front of us. "If they're really upping the game to get us out, we could see if any of the others have any ideas?"

Eirlys nodded. "I'll let you know what I hear. In the meantime, I'm not letting that bad news sleeze anywhere near my shop."

Focusing on the rest of the lesson, my mind ran a mile a minute. What could we actually do that would make a difference? Catch him in the act? That could work. If there was proof, the owner of the rink would have to kick them out.

A tiny head butted my right leg. Asher was standing on the flat of my foot looking up at me. Could a goat smirk?

"Yes, Ash?" My lips twitched as I held back the smile.

Asher narrowed his eyes at me, his tail went up, and he started dropping little poop balls on my mat.

"Really? Aren't I supposed to be your favorite?" My glare didn't phase him at all. Little shit. Literally.

That was the end of class for me. Luckily, Maya ended it after a few more minutes.

"Great job everyone. Kids, clean up the messes you

made. Asher, don't think I didn't see what you did. You better apologize." Maya used her 'mom' voice.

Ha! Served him right. There was a reason Riley was my favorite.

"Cider, could I talk to you after this?" Titus was behind me, his head tilted forward.

My body instantly relaxed. I pressed into his front without thought.

"Always, big guy."

His hands rested on my shoulders and I'm pretty sure I felt how happy he was to be pressed against me. His eyes certainly eluded to what he was thinking.

Oh boy. It had just gotten hotter in this place.

"Hold it, Titus. Before you go all yuck on her." Eirlys rolled up her mat. "Cider, thank you for the invite to this. It was nice to just relax. I'll talk to some of the other store owners and get back to you. And Cider? My friends call me Lys."

We shook hands. Which was a huge step considering we hated each other last month. She dragged my brother away with Jace and Fallon.

"Now that those idiots and my daughter are gone." Titus squeezed my shoulders. "Let's have that talk in my truck?"

I said goodbye to the kids and Maya. We made plans for dinner next week at her place before I walked out to the cars with my vampire mate at my side.

"So?" I looked up at him. The man was tall.

He opened the back door to his truck. His hands went to my waist, picked me up, and set me inside before I could blink. He was next to me with the door shut in the next second.

"I wanted some alone time with you." His hand cupped my chin, his touch setting me on fire.

"I like that idea." My mumble was cut off as his lips met mine. "Mmm!"

My hands were everywhere. Running over his shoulders, his chest, down his legs to cup his hardened cock.

Titus rumbled, rocking his hips into my hand. "Gods, I can't think when you're touching me."

Squeezing his member, I moved to push down his pants, pulling it out.

"Feelings mutual." I could barely form words as I ran my fingers down him. He was hard, soft, and hot all at once.

"Wait." He gripped my wrist gently as he pulled my hands above my head. "Keep your hands up. I'm not going to last long our first time, my dear. I'm about to burst." His words were breathless as I noticed he was shaking with pent up lust. "Let me get you ready."

He kissed me roughly for several seconds before moving downward. I moved my hips so he could pull my pants and panties off, throwing them over his shoulder somewhere.

He didn't give me time to say anything before his fingers were spreading my pussy lips apart and his tongue flicked out at my clit.

Titus drove two fingers inside of my aching pussy at the same time he wrapped his lips around my sensitive bud, sucking as if his life depended on sucking my soul out of my body.

My fingers wrapped tightly in his hair as I clenched my thighs around his shoulders, pushing my pussy as close to him as I could get. I was just on the edge of my climax when he pulled his mouth and fingers from me.

I hissed angrily at that but he just chuckled.

"Patience, my little fox." He removed my legs around

his shoulders, wrapping them around his waist, pressing his cock into my folds as he leaned forward to kiss my neck. "Don't forget to breathe."

Then he bit down, sinking his teeth into my flesh. My orgasm ripped through me as he surged inside of my pussy. His hips thrust so hard, he pushed us up the seats.

My hands hit the back window as I groped for some kind of holding as he drank my blood and fucked me into oblivion in the back seat of his truck.

His hands dug into my ass from where he held me up as he used his strength to fuck us both to completion. When my pussy tightened around his cock, he groaned and I felt him jerk as he came.

It took some time for my breath to steady. Holy vampire balls.

"Wow." My giggle slipped out before I could stop it. "We should talk more."

Titus nuzzled my neck with his nose. Licking at the spot he'd bitten. I shivered.

"Oh, we can talk all day and night if you wanted." His chuckle made me laugh.

"Pretty sure Maya is going to notice your truck just sitting outside of her house. And my car." I pushed at his shoulders as I looked for my panties.

"That's probably a good point." He handed me the piece of clothing that had somehow gotten caught on the headrest of the driver's seat. "So, I'll see you at dinner tonight?"

My clothes were back on, if a little rumpled. "Yes, dinner tonight. Is the asshole coming?"

Titus nodded as he hopped out of the back of the truck, lifting me out. I never knew getting lifted by hands on the waist would be so hot, but it was.

"Yes, Jack is coming. He feels bad for the way he acted. He plans on making up for it." Titus kissed the top of my left hand gently. "I look forward to meeting Billy."

He held open my car door and shut it. I watched him walk back to his truck, a little dazed. That had just happened. I wasn't sure if I should tell Maya that I'd had sex in her front of her house in a car. Maybe in a few years.

CHAPTER 11

"Is this right?" I stepped back and stared at the potatoes that I'd been smashing with the tool that Billy had handed to me. "They are still all chunky."

"That's fine." Billy looked at the bowl over my shoulder. "I have a feeling that our guests like chunky." His snicker was interrupted when I smacked him in the stomach. "Hey! It's true!"

I shook my head. "You are really going for a record for really bad jokes or pick-up lines, aren't you?" I handed him the mashed potatoes.

"Yes. Yes, I am." My best friend winked outrageously as he took the bowl to the table. "I'm interested in meeting your other mates. Titus seems like one of those guys we used to make fun of at school. The rich, haughty taughty like. At least, that's the impression I got when he talked to me on the phone before." His tone was teasing, so I knew he wasn't being mean.

"Titus is, well, Titus? I'm not sure how to describe him. He's just, yum?" My tongue became confused as I thought of the way he'd gone down on me in the back of his truck earlier in the day. "Man knows what he's doing at least."

Billy raised an eyebrow. "Ha! I knew it! You smelled like sex when you came home."

I scrunched my nose at him. "Why are you smelling me? I went right to take a shower."

Billy walked over and wrapped his arms around my back, pulling me up against his chest. "Because you smell good. You're my mate. You're mine." That last one he growled into my ear and my knees wobbled.

"You ass. You know growling is my weakness!" I tried to be stern, but it came out weak and pathetic. Billy looked far too proud of himself as he held me from falling on my butt.

"I just never thought I would get to use it on you." His grin just got bigger.

"I'm going to tell your sister you're picking on me." I stepped to the side, albeit a little wobbly.

"We both know Maya will tell you to suck my dick to shut me up." He turned back to the oven.

The asshat was right. She totally would. I licked my lips. That wouldn't be a bad idea. Would be fun to get back at Billy for his joke, too.

I glanced at the clock on the wall. We still had about twenty minutes before the other two guys were scheduled to arrive. That was plenty of time.

I snuck up behind Billy and my arms went around his waist, my fingers rubbed under his waistband. His growl grumbled through his body.

"Cider." He put down the spatula he'd been using. "What are you doing?"

I pushed his waistband down, over his hips, and down far enough I could stick my hand in his boxers. He was already semi-hard.

"I'm not sure." I pressed my lips to his arm as my hand stroked down his length slowly. My thumb rubbed his head, spreading the drop of cum that had already started to form at my touch. "Maybe you should turn around so I can continue."

I didn't even finish the sentence and he'd turned around, his hands running down my arms.

"Baby, you don't need to do this." His gruff voice was soft.

I knelt in front of him, pulling down his boxers to his knees. "Oh, yes, I do."

His cock stood up with its red tip. My right hand cupped his length, moving with slow strokes as my left fondled his balls. His soft hiss was all I needed to hear to know I was doing it right.

Who knew that I'd love sucking my best friend's cock so much?

I couldn't take him all the way into my mouth, but I gave it my best shot. He seemed to really enjoy it when I ran my tongue on the underside of his cock.

"Ughn, Cider. You've got to stop, I'm going to burst." Billy dug his fingers into my hair. I was thankful it was down so he didn't pull too hard.

I just kept sucking on his shaft. He seemed to realize I was going to take him all the way. His fingers tightened and his hips jerked a few times as he fought to hold himself still while I pleasured him.

A few minutes passed as I picked up the speed. His groan was the only heads up I had before he came inside my mouth.

It wasn't too unpleasant. I swallowed as he pulled away from me. His fingers touched my chin, he looked about to say something.

The doorbell rang. I started to giggle as Billy pulled up his shorts and handed me a washcloth.

"I'll go let them in." Billy kissed me roughly as he walked toward the door.

Mmm. That man. Took a mating bond to snap into place for me to finally admit that I loved watching his ass.

"Welcome to our home." Billy led Titus and a grouchy looking Jack Frost inside.

Titus was wearing a fitted black suit that made my mouth water. Jack was wearing sweats, his hair was messy, and he was glaring at me.

"Cider, you look divine." Titus stepped forward, his arms lifted me from the ground as he hugged me. His nose moved behind my ear and I could hear his smile. "You smell even better with a mix of goat." He pulled back and winked at Billy.

My mountain man blushed as he cleared his throat. My grin hurt my face as he started bringing the food to the table. His whole face was red and he refused to look at Titus.

Oh my God. I looked between them and my hands tingled with the need to clap them together. Was that sexual tension between them? Please, let it be. This perverted fox totally loved her some man on man love.

"Thanks for having us." Titus' low voice rolled over my senses.

"Sure." Billy cleared his throat as he finished bringing out the food. "I hope you don't mind vegetarian dishes."

I sat next to Billy as Titus sat next to Jack across from us.

"I'm fine with vegetarian. I had my red blood earlier this afternoon." Titus licked his lower bottom while staring at me.

Oh boy. It was getting hotter in here as my cheeks filled with blood.

"Do you ever keep it in your pants?" Jack gave a side glare to Titus. "It's been centuries and you still flirt with anything with a pulse. *Even her.*" His gaze found mine and I went pale.

Before I could reply to his insult, Titus was standing over him with Jack's face pressed into the table with Titus' hand on his neck.

"Now, Jack, you and I have known each other for a very long time, but I've never known you to be intentionally hurtful. Especially to a woman that is your mate. Our mate."

Shit. Titus was so getting laid after dinner. This was so much better than my idea of throwing the bowl of mashed potatoes at Jack's face.

"Now, apologize to Cider, and if you can't say anything nice, don't open your mouth. Got it?" he growled into Jack's ear before pushing away from him. He sat back at the table, put a napkin on his lap, and looked up as if he didn't just go alphahole on Jack.

Jack's hair was standing up as he ran his hands through it. He wouldn't look me in the eyes.

"Titus is right, I'm sorry. That was rude."

Even though he was a dick, he still made my body stand up at his voice. My tits were traitors.

"Thanks." I glanced at Billy, who looked murderous. "Why don't we eat?"

Besides a few awkward minutes, dinner went swimmingly. Jack actually ended up talking and being a reasonable person. He was also funny.

Dang it. It was hard to stay mad at the guy when he made me laugh so hard, water came out my nose.

Billy had loosened up and looked to be enjoying himself. Titus was, well, Titus.

It was coming on to two AM when Jack pushed himself from the table as he stood.

"Thank you for the company and dinner. It was... enlightening." He nodded at Billy before looking at me. "I'm sorry, again. I'll speak with you later." With that, he left, shutting the front door behind him quietly.

"I think he just needed his head knocked around a little. He's always been like that. Stubborn and assholeish until someone clocked him." Titus rubbed his jaw, a small smile across his face. "He's actually quite charming underneath that cool exterior." He winked at me. "I guess that's my cue that I should head out."

"Wait." Billy spoke before I could. "You don't have to leave, if you want to stay the night. That is, if Cider is alright with it?" His face was deep red.

Oh. Hell. Yes.

I was totally getting some man on man love. My fox's tail shook in excitement.

Titus had frozen as Billy spoke. His eyes roamed over Billy's face, narrowing as he contemplated the invitation.

"You don't have to do anything." Billy started to panic. "It's totally fine! I can stay in my room." He held up his hands.

Titus moved from around the table to stand in front of Billy. They weren't the same height, yet the way he moved, he seemed somehow bigger. He reached out to run a finger up Billy's neck that stopped him from his blabbering that he'd continued while Titus had walked over to him.

"Billy," Titus' voice was silk. "I would be more than happy to get to know you just as intimately as we know our mate."

I watched, wide eyed, as Titus brushed his finger down Billy's front before he kissed him. Billy stiffened, briefly, before his mouth opened under Titus' assault. Titus pulled Billy against him as his hands gripped the back of Billy's ass.

The sound of Billy panting brought my eyes back up. Titus had moved from his mouth and was kissing a line down his neck to his collarbone. Billy's hands clutched Titus' shoulders, white knuckled. Billy's eyes were closed as he tipped his head back, letting Titus have easier access to his neck.

Titus growled at the sign of submission, running his tongue along Billy's Adam's apple, which made Billy visibly shiver. Titus' hands moved from clutching Billy's ass. He started pulling off Billy's shirt, only pulling his mouth from the spot he was sucking on his collar to throw the shirt across the room. Billy started pulling at Titus' shirt when the vampire stepped away.

"We should put away the food you made us, we wouldn't want it to go to waste, now, would we?" His deep voice was filled with mirth. He knew he was torturing Billy and wasn't apologizing for it.

Billy looked confused, it was actually pretty damn cute. The sexual frustration that I was feeling, I could only imagine what it felt like for Billy.

"I can clean up." Offering to move the things to the fridge was the least I could do for Billy. "You two can head to the room and continue."

"Oh, sweet, Cider." Titus smirked at me. "Don't think that I've forgotten about you." He placed a palm on Billy's chest, making him back up toward the hallway. "Hurry up, my fox. We have a horny goat to pleasure."

They disappeared from sight and that's all I needed to

kick my butt into gear. The dining room table was cleared in record time, the food placed in the fridge, and the dishes put in a sink full of hot water and soap.

I practically sprinted to the back where the rooms were. Titus had gone into the first room, which was mine. I stumbled to a stop as I clutched the doorframe.

Billy was spread out on the bed with his knees bent, clutching my headboard, his clothes look like they'd been torn in half on the floor, with Titus' mouth around his cock.

Oh, hot tamales.

Titus was sucking his cock like a champion who knew what he was doing. His left hand trailed up Billy's chest, his nails scratching Billy's chest hair roughly. He tweaked Billy's left nipple as his lips pulled off of his cock.

Titus glanced at me with hooded eyes.

"Hello, baby. Come over here." His command sent my pussy into override. "Be a good girl and straddle Billy."

My pants and underwear were lost by the time I'd made it to the bed. Titus was on his knees, his shirt was unbuttoned, and his pants were pushed down. His hand stroked his cock as he watched me move to him.

"Take his cock into you." Titus guided me as I threw my leg over Billy, positioning myself over his dick, facing him. "You're going to ride him while I lick you and him."

My pussy tightened in anticipation. Billy met my gaze and his gaze was filled with lust. Titus' hands rested on my waist as he pushed me down on top of Billy's cock.

"Oh, fuck!" My hands rested on Billy's knees as his cock moved inside of me. Titus' hands stayed on my waist as I felt him shift.

Then there was a swipe of a hot tongue along my pussy. By Billy's moan, the tongue was also licking his cock.

Titus' hands tightened on my hips and he started

moving me on top of Billy's cock. My gasp was loud as Titus moved my hips faster and faster. Billy grasped the front of my hips as he began slamming up into me at the same time.

With the friction from Billy's cock and Titus' tongue, I was close to losing my mind. The pressure built as both men made me lose it. I cried out when Titus' tongue pushed into my pussy along with Billy's cock and I came hard.

Billy was right behind, his orgasm making him grunt. He pulled me forward into his chest to kiss me. I rolled over on my side as the hands on my back moved to my hair. Titus moved, curling around me and Billy. He pulled my chin, stopping my kiss with Billy. He leaned forward to kiss him than me.

"Beautiful." His gravelly voice made my toes curl.

CHAPTER 12

"What do you mean you're sold out?" My voice squeaked, echoing in my small store before opening.

I'd been in such a good mood waking up that morning. It had been a little over a week since the dinner with all my mates. Everything was going great between Billy, Titus, and I. Things were slowly moving forward with Jack.

Now, my good mood turned foul.

I'd had to reorder supplies, including my secret ingredient for my cider drink, and the suppliers were out of stock. Just like Lys had mentioned. I hadn't thought it would be this bad, though. Even the local grocery store was out of most of the things I needed.

"Sorry, we won't have replacement stock for another week." The man was apologetic, but there wasn't anything he could do.

I placed the phone in the cradle before rubbing my temples. I didn't have enough stock to last a week. I'd have to go out of town to other grocery stores to see if I could find any of the supplies.

The door opened. I glanced up to say that we were still closed when my mouth snapped back.

Samuel walked in. He looked like he'd bathed in oil with his hair smoothed down. He ran his fingers along one of the tables.

He'd been slinking around the rink lately while construction continued on his store.

"Hello, Cider." He glanced at his fingers before rubbing them on his shirt. "I hoped you would have a few minutes to discuss a proposal."

I tried not to wince at the slimy feeling he gave off. I was glad I was behind the counter.

"I'm sorry?" My lips pressed together as he got closer.

"Well, we're expanding our menu to reflect the rink. I've noticed your shop is fairly popular." His compliment sounded like an insult.

"Thanks?" My fingers grew claws and I had to hide them under the counter.

"How would you feel about sharing your recipes with us? They'll be featured nationwide with your brand." He stood on the other side of the counter. He withdrew papers from his inner coat and placed it in front of me. "This would be your contract. You'd only have to close this shop and work exclusively with Darcorp, creating more of these delicious concoctions."

This guy had balls. Breathing in deeply, I forced my claws back.

"The offer is appreciated." No, it wasn't. "I'll have to decline." I pushed the paper back to him.

Samuel took a step back without picking up the paper. "I was curious. Have you happened to hear about my car?"

I blinked innocently. "No. What happened?"

He narrowed his eyes. "Someone thought it would be

funny to prank me." He shook his head. "Think about it for a few days." He backed himself to the door. "It might be your only option soon."

With that ominous statement, he left. I blinked, confused for a few moments. I picked up the paper and noticed a sticky note in the middle.

It read: *Sign soon. Supplies and stock will be missing for a long while.*

My curses filled the room. I grabbed the phone and dialed Triple E.

"Triple—"

I interrupted. "This weasel just basically admitted to buying up all the stock and left me a note about it! He wants me to sign over my recipes."

Glancing over the paper that held his offer, I grunted in annoyance. The offer was insulting, too. It would barely cover the loan I had to take out to get the shop started.

"Wait. He actually came into your store and offered to buy you out?" Lys sounded like someone had punched her in the gut.

"Oh, not even that. Just to buy my recipes. I'd have to shut down my store if I accepted. Which I am not going to accept. It's a disgusting offer. Plus, the whole note about the missing stock!" I started to pace behind the counter. "We have to stop this guy and Darcorp. It's not just going to be my place they go after."

"I'm going to talk to Titus. See if he has any ideas on what we can do. In the meantime, everyone's going to need stock soon. I think Titus might be able to help with that, too. He uses a separate supplier for his lodge than we use in town."

I stopped in mid step. "He does? Lodge?"

"Oh, you don't know?" I could practically see the knowing grin she had to have. "He owns Sanguis Vinum."

Shit. Sanguis Vinum was a fancy resort for supernaturals that wanted to get away from humans. It was pricey. I'd wanted to go there for years to run through the woods without fear of running into a human.

And one of my mates owned it. Would it be bad to drop hints at him that I wanted to go away with him for a weekend there? It would. Right?

"Cider?" Lys brought my attention back to the phone call. "You alright there?"

"Yeah, I was just thinking."

There was the sound of scuffling before Quinten's voice came on the line.

"Couldn't have been that hard since there's nothing in there."

My eyelid twitched. "Seriously? How juvenile are you?"

"That's what she said." Quinten yelped. "Ow! Lys!"

"Stop being a child!" I listened in amusement as the other line hung up.

We'd have to finish our conversation later. For now, I needed to open the store and focus on what I could do in the moment.

Including making a note to call Igor for her ideas. Now, it had gotten personal.

CHAPTER 13

The zamboni had been on the ice multiple times today because of the hockey team's practice. That meant I was able to watch Jack as he concentrated on driving around the strange machine. A few times, I'd even caught him looking at my store's direction.

There had to be a story there. He'd been cruel when our bond had formed and that night had been even worse when he'd come over for our first dinner. Yet, when Titus had chastised him, he'd snapped out of whatever funk he'd been. Those two had history, I remembered that Titus had mentioned that, but there had to be more.

Because of the practice, I was busy throughout the day. Fans liked to come watch the Silver Springs team whenever they were on the ice. Even if it wasn't an actual game. By the time closing came around, most patrons of the rink were heading out.

I had just been about to head out when the door opened to admit Jack inside. His hair was windblown and there were snowflakes on his eyelashes.

My breath caught as he shook out his hair with his hand. He looked up at me and froze.

"Hi." A giggle slipped out at the simple greeting.

His lips curled in a smile that took the rest of the air out of my lungs. "Hi."

We both laughed for several long moments. It helped ease the tension.

"Cider." Jack sombered first. "What are you doing tomorrow night?"

Out of the scenarios that ran through my head, that question had not been part of any of them. I'd even had one where I threw a cup at his face.

"Tomorrow night? Nothing. I think? Should I?" I stepped around the counter, closer to him.

He met me halfway, surprising me. He looked down at me with his hooded eyes that sent my blood boiling and my nipples betrayed me again.

"I owe you an explanation for the way I've treated you. Can I take you on a date?" He held his hands together, the only thing showing that he was nervous.

"Yes." I didn't even have to think about it. "Only if you'll let me make you a drink sometime."

There was that devastating smile again.

"Deal. Make sure you wear warm clothing, okay?" Jack placed a hand on my shoulder, squeezed it, and walked out. "See you tomorrow!"

My heart warm, I didn't pay much attention as I locked the door and headed to my car. I didn't see the note that was under my wipers until I'd actually gotten into my car and started it.

"Damnit," I got back out of the car, grabbed it, and got back inside. I locked the doors before opening the note.

My mouth dropped. It was a single word, but that word was my secret ingredient to my hot cider drink.

"Son of a bitch!" Slapping my hands on the steering wheel, I started cursing up a storm again.

It had to be Samuel. He was the only one who had any interest in it. But how did he figure it out? I didn't have it written down. It was all in my head. Plus, I used the secret ingredient in several other drinks, so it's not like anyone could figure it out.

Feeling a sense of dread, I backed out of the parking space and headed home. I was a little scared at that moment and needed to get back to Billy since he'd be home.

Thankfully, all the lights on the outside were on as I hurriedly went in.

Billy was sitting at the island sipping a drink. From the smell, it was whiskey. His hair was slicked back, still wet from a shower.

"Hey, Cid." He turned as I locked the door. "What's wrong?" His eyes narrowed.

I hadn't even needed to say anything and he figured out I was upset. Years of friendship at work.

I handed him the two notes from Samuel and the offer that he'd given me. As he read them, his free hand that held the drink clenched, cracking the top of the glass. He placed it back on the island.

"What is this, Cid?" Billy placed the papers next to the broken glass before pulling me between his legs with his arms around my back.

"Samuel, the guy from Darcorp, stopped by the store today. That note with the secret ingredient was on my car when I left work." I took a deep breath as I lay my head on his chest. His steady heartbeat was comforting with the smell of fresh cut grass that was Billy. "This guy is serious. He's actually trying to kick me out." The tears were threatening to fall, but I refused to let them. I wouldn't let a parasite like Samuel win.

One of Billy's hands stroked my hair down my back as the other tightened around my waist. Just being near him helped my stress melt away.

"He can't do this." His voice held a note of anger in it. Billy didn't usually get angry. "We'll figure this out." His lips pressed to my forehead. "You've worked too hard to get where you are now."

"Thanks, Billbill." His childhood nickname just slipped out as he held me. "Billy," I looked up into his eyes. "Are you alright? With everything that's happened?"

His lips tugged up. "You mean the part where, I, as a straight man, let another man suck my dick and make out with me the other night?"

Snorting, I nodded. "Yeah, that."

His shrug was nonchalant. "It happened. Am I surprised about it? Hell, yes. Do I regret it? No way. That man has a tongue of sin. Will I do more than that with him? I'm not sure. I don't want a dick inside of me anytime soon, that's for sure." He pushed some hair behind my ear that had fallen forward as he teased me. "You obviously enjoyed it."

"It was probably the hottest thing that I've ever seen." My confession got another grin from him. "But, I don't want you to do anything that you're not comfortable with. I know that Titus will respect your boundaries."

I actually didn't, but Titus was a gentleman that I doubted who would over step boundaries that were laid down.

Billy's chest moved again, but this time he laughed. "You know, you're right. For some reason, without knowing the guy, I was instantly attracted to him, and trusted him." He pulled back, standing from the stool. "Come on. Let's go cuddle on the couch and watch some cheesy romantic comedies. That always cheers you up when we can make fun of the unrealistic acts." His hand held mine gently as we moved to the living room.

"Did you know that Titus is the owner of Sanguis Vinum?" I settled into the oversized couch cushions that practically ate a person.

Billy pulled me so that I was laying half on him. This was new and I loved it.

"No shit?" He turned on the television and started surfing through the channels. "Looks like we need to take advantage of his sexy ass. Maybe he'll let us come visit in exchange for blowjobs?"

My burst of laughter was muffled as I buried my head in his neck. "Oh my God. How bad is it that I thought that at first, too?"

Billy winked as he settled on a movie about a bartender who could see and speak with ghosts. It wasn't a romantic comedy, but it was one of my all time favorites.

"Maybe Titus will have an idea about this Samuel guy." Billy's hand rubbing my back was putting me to sleep.

"That's a good idea." My yawn interrupted me.

"Take a nap, Cid. I'm not going anywhere. We can figure it out once you wake up." Billy's gentle voice lulled me to sleep.

CHAPTER 14

"...Yeah. That's what she told me." Billy's voice filtered through my sleep laden brain. "Yeah. She'll be thankful. How much is the extra charge, though?"

I had a hard time opening my eyes. I was so comfortable.

Billy snorted. "She's going to have a few things to say about that. She doesn't like hand outs." Billy gulped and shifted, which made me shift since I was laying on him still. I felt him harden.

That woke me up faster. I rested my chin on his chest as I looked up into his face as he talked on the phone. His eyes met mine and they visibly softened. I liked that.

"Hey, she's awake. Talk to her." Billy spoke into the phone quickly before he placed it against my ear, waiting for me to take it from him. "It's Titus."

"Titus?" My voice cracked. I needed water.

"Bellissimo." Titus' voice sent delicious shivers through me. "Billy was just catching me up on what happened. I spoke with little Snowdrop earlier as well."

"Mmm." I was still in that blissful sensation when you wake up and feel like you're floating.

Titus chuckled, his voice softened. "Still not awake, my fox? Do I need to come over and wake you up with my tongue in your pussy?"

Okay. I was awake for that. I pushed off against Billy's chest, making him grunt.

"That was not fair." Hissing into the phone, I ran a hand through my hair that was standing up on its own. I snagged on some of it.

"Oh, but it was worth it." Titus was down right gleeful. "Now, I've got my supplier delivering emergency stock to the stores in the rink, minus Darcorp. Billy told me what you needed."

"What? How did you manage that? How much is this supplier?" I was doing okay at the store, with a little saved up, but I didn't have a lot of extra savings to pay for an out of town supplier.

"It won't cost you a dime, my sweets." His voice was distracting.

"I'm not letting you pay for my stock." I stood from the couch. "That's not how this relationship is going to start out with." I started pacing.

"Told you." Billy's voice was loud enough for Titus to hear through the phone.

"Now, Cider." His tone was chidding. "You're running a business. You can't really pick and choose if this helps you not lose out on business."

I could feel the twitches start coming on. "Yes, I do. You didn't even ask me if that was okay for you to do!"

There was a brief moment of silence.

"Forgive me, Cider. I've not had a lover in a long time where I actually wanted to take care of them and love them as I do you. I've just had my daughter to care for the past few years. I overstepped. Will you please allow me to assist in this matter?" His apology made my fur stand down.

"Well, when you put it like that." My shoulders slumped as Billy started covering his laughter by coughing. "I might have overreacted."

"No, sweet fox, you're an independent woman. And have been for some time." I heard the smile in his voice. "It will be interesting to see how we butt heads, as it were, in the future." He certainly had a silver tongue. I guess that made sense because he was a silver fox.

I snickered to myself at the horrible joke.

"Now, about this Samuel." Titus interrupted my internal monologuing. "I am curious to find out how he found out that information. Billy said that you don't have it written down anywhere? What about accidentally writing a list down for shopping? Notice any new scents around the house?"

My head cocked to the side as I thought over the last few days. I hadn't noticed anything out of the ordinary. Billy shook his head as he looked at me.

"No, neither of us."

"How intriguing." Titus was now mumbling to himself. "Let me see what I can find out."

"Oh! Titus, before you hang up." I needed to tell him.

"Yes, my sweet?"

Damn his voice was smooth and velvety over my skin.

"Jack asked me out on a date tomorrow night." I looked at Billy as I said it so that he knew he was included in the conversation.

Billy frowned but didn't say anything. There was clapping from the other side of the phone.

"Thatta boy. Finally got that stick that he'd shoved up

his ass loose. Enjoy your date tomorrow. If you need me, you have my number. I'll see you soon." Titus said his goodnight so that Billy could hear and we hung up.

"Are you sure about that guy?" Billy crossed his arms across his chest.

Shrugging, I moved so that I could flop down across his lap. "Yeah. I think there's more under the cold exterior that he was hiding. Whatever Titus did, it seems to have snapped him out of whatever funk he was in." I turned to look at the television. "How about a movie before bed? This time, I won't fall asleep, promise."

"Yeah, right. You always fall asleep." Billy picked up the remote and handed it to me anyway.

We both ended up falling asleep about a third of the way through the movie. When we woke up in the morning to my phone's alarm, I growled.

"You have the most annoying alarm." Billy pushed me off his lap, making me roll across the cushions. "Holy crud. Cider, I'm going to be late! I call shower first." He was up and gone before I could even blink my eyes.

My fox whined at me. She wanted to run again. I glanced at the time. I didn't have time to do that today but made plans to go for a run the next day, which seemed to settle her.

That's when I remembered. I had a date tonight.

"BILLY! I get the shower first! I've got to get ready for work and my date tonight!" I scrambled over the couch, because going around it made no sense, and ran for the bathroom. "You take forever to groom your beard!"

The door was already locked. I banged on it as Billy started to sing The Goat Song from the shower.

"Goats are clever. Goats are wise. They've got four legs, they've got two eyes. Goats eat anything from fillet steak to oats...." Billy belted out the notes as if he were in front of an audience.

"Dang it, Billy!" I slapped the door as he laughed on the other side.

I'd just have to figure it out on the fly. I sniffed my armpit as I started going through my clean clothes in the closet.

Well, at least I didn't reek. I could clean up a tiny bit in the back of the store later if I started to.

My phone dinged with a text from Titus.

Good morning, my heart. I hope you have fun tonight.

I couldn't stop the joyous feeling that spread through me as I pulled on clean clothes.

Morning, fangboy. I'll let you know how it goes. He might run since I don't have time to take a shower because a certain goat is hogging the shower.

There was an instant reply. Dang, he typed fast.

You'll smell just as divine as you usually do. I've got a meeting. I'll talk to you later.

My phone went into my front pocket of the jeans I pulled on with a few hops to get over the stomach. They were a little fancy since they had black glitter in the fabric. I decided to leave my hair down after brushing through it. I even put on a little dab of clear lip gloss.

Oh man. I had it bad. I wanted Jack to like me. The matebond was there pushing us together, but I really did want to get to know him. He seemed like he could use a friend.

There were no signs of Samuel, at least, when I got to the rink. I was actually a few minutes early. I really needed to work on getting up earlier.

Igor was standing outside of the door, relaxing against

the wood. She was watching a group of kids play tag a little down the way.

"Hey, Igor." I unlocked the door, letting her through before closing it and locking it again. "What's up?"

Igor seemed upset as she started to walk between the tables. She pulled down the chairs.

"Lawrence isn't talking to me. He says that I'm selfish." She put a chair down so hard, it almost cracked the tiled floor. "Would a selfish person come in and help you for free?"

I bit my lip to stop from laughing. I was pretty sure if I laughed at her right now, she'd eat me.

"What were you doing when he called you selfish?" I put my personal things under the counter.

"I was making a list of things I wanted done once I dominated this town. Specifically, the greenhouse. I wanted a larger place to spread out at night. I was thinking of taking over that orphanage's place." She sat on the other side of the counter.

I could feel my face pale. "Uh, you do know the mafia protects that area, right?"

She waved her hand. "Like I'm afraid of a few furballs. It's the perfect location for optimal sunbathing."

Oh boy. "Have you talked to Iris about this?"

"No. That harlot and her slaves are off on some adventure in the desert. Left me in charge for the next week." Igor thumped her hands on the counter. "That's selfish!"

It was fascinating sometimes to remember that Igor wasn't like the rest of us. She wasn't human, or a supernatural technically. She had a lot to learn.

"Well, where would the orphans go if you took their home?"

She glared at her hands. "Lawrence asked the same thing and got mad when I said I didn't care."

I flicked her in the forehead. "Take a second to reflect on that statement."

She rubbed her forehead as she hissed at me but she didn't immediately reply. That meant she was actually thinking about it. I went about prepping to open while she did.

I'd just unlocked the door and flipped the sign to open when she spoke.

"I'm selfish because I didn't think about where kids, who don't have parents already, would go if I took away their home?" Her tough attitude had momentarily vanished. In its place, was a young vulnerable woman who didn't know what empathy meant.

"It's a selfish idea, yes." I handed her a cup before pouring some cooled apple cider. "Maybe look for land that doesn't have buildings on it for your plans? That could show Lawrence you thought about what he said."

She took a sip before nodding. "You're right. I need to start thinking about things besides how they will work in my favor." She set the now empty cup down. "I had a thought on your problem. What if I follow him around for a few days? I can see if I can find anything to use against him that wouldn't involve actually eating him."

Pausing for a second. I thought about it. Normally, I wouldn't want to involve a friend, but she offered and if anyone could get information without getting caught, it would be Igor. No one noticed a random plant. This guy was gunning for my livelihood and pranks really weren't going to cut it.

"Let's do it."

Igor grinned, her teeth had sharpened to points. Oh boy.

As Igor left for the day, I focused on the next customers that started coming through. The steady stream of customers helped keep my mind occupied from the date that would be happening in a few short hours.

CHAPTER 15

Closing time finally came and went. I was in the back fixing my hair when a knock at the front brought me out. It was time.

I smoothed my hand down my shirt as I came back from the back. Jack had his right knuckles raised against the glass. I paused to take him in.

Woah. He was wearing skin tight clothes, no hoodie in sight. His hair was styled up. His skin was dark against the light which made his eyes stand out even more.

He opened the door as soon as I unlocked it.

"Hey." He took my hand. "Thank you for giving me a second chance. You look beautiful." Our fingers twined together naturally.

I closed the door, locking it quickly with my other hand. I wasn't letting go of Jack's unless he did.

"I can't wait to spend time with you." Looking up at him, I couldn't help but stare at him a little dazed. He was actually really pretty for a man. He tried to hide it under all the baggy clothes he wore.

His pleased look was soft. "I don't usually hear

that. In case you haven't noticed, I'm a little bit of a dick to pretty much everyone. The grump of the rink."

He started walking toward the rink, pulling me along with him as I pocketed my keys.

"Everyone's entitled to be an asshole once in a while." Shrugging, I glanced around.

It looked like pretty much everyone had left. The lights around the rink flickered on as we approached it.

In the middle of the ice, there was a table set up with two foldable chairs facing each other. There was a black table cloth and candles that were already lit. Two plates were covered by silver domes.

I stopped and Jack paused with me. When I looked up at him, he looked to the side sheepishly, as if embarrassed. The tips of his ears looked like they turned a deep red off the lighting was any indication.

"Jack." I squeezed his hand which made him look back at me. "Thank you. It's beautiful."

"Watch your step." Jack watched my feet as we made our way across the ice. It wasn't nearly as hard as I thought it was going to be.

I thought I would slip for sure--- And there it was.

I started to slip, my fox freaking out, but my ass never met the ice. An arm wrapped around my waist, pulling me up against a very impressive hard chest.

"Careful." Jack's voice held a sultry note. He had to be feeling what I was. It was like his touch sent electrical signals to every part of my body. It was ready to go with him.

Right there. On the ice.

Oh boy.

We got to the table and Jack pulled out the chair for me.

When I sat, he easily slid it in. I grabbed the napkin and fanned my face.

"Did it suddenly get hot here?" I looked around.

Jack sat across from me, and I swear to God, he gave me a Flynn Ryder smoulder. Yup. My ovaries were now awake and raring to go.

"We're in the middle of an ice rink. Pretty sure it's actually cold." He held up a finger. "If you'd like it to be colder, I'd be happy to help. After all, I am the Winter King."

It began to snow. Not the spelled snow that the area usually had, but actual snow. Big flakes fell softly around us but it didn't touch us. It was like there was a bubble of air around us that the snow fell around. It was beautiful against the dark sky and the lights around us.

Jack removed the covers on the plates and the smell of steak made my fox growl in hunger.

"Oh, dang. This looks amazing." My fox whined.

"I liked the food at your place, but I have to confess," Jack picked up his fork and knife, "I'm more of a pink meat eater myself." He kept his eyes locked with mine as he cut a piece, chewed it slowly, and swallowed.

My laughter spilled out over the area. My stomach jiggled with how hard I laughed.

"Are you referring to my pussy as red meat?" I was having a hard time getting the words out.

That's when he did it.

Jack laughed. He threw his head back and laughed in delight.

"I guess I am. Was it really that bad of a pick up line?"

I shook my head, grabbing the napkin again, this time to dab at the corner of my eyes where I'd actually started to cry.

"It was bad. Not in a bad way. But, yeah, that was bad. You and Billy will get along swimmingly."

"I'm a little rusty at all of this." His look of happiness made me want to melt. I just wanted to keep watching him. "I've not had a proper date, or relationship, in centuries. I don't think you could call what Titus and I have a relationship."

I'd just picked up my fork. "What do you mean?" Please, say lovers.

"We're fuck buddies." His bluntness was refreshing.

SCORE! Maybe they'd let me watch. Well, I knew Titus would.

I took a bite of the steak and had to swallow the moan that wanted to come out.

"I see." Trying to appear nonchalant was killing me. If my tail was out, it would be wagging like a dogs. "Will you continue to be 'fuck buddies'?"

Jack moved his head to the left, exposing the side of his neck. Those veins were impressive and I had to resist the urge to bite him, to mark him as mine. Somehow, the idea of diving over the table seemed like a bad idea while we were on a blanket of ice.

"I guess that would depend on you." He started to eat his dinner again. I noticed that he cut precise pieces of whatever he was eating.

"If I said no?" There was no way in the nine hells that I would say that.

I watched his expression carefully. If I hadn't been, I'd have missed the flicker of sadness that flashed in his eyes before it disappeared.

"I would respect that since you're my mate." His answer was almost robotic.

Man, I had hit a nerve. My fox purred in triumph. Oh, this would be fun. There was no harm in teasing him.

"That's good." I took another bite of steak. Damn. It was good. I'd have to ask who made it and see if I could order from them. "I mean, I have to tell you."

Jack had looked down at his plate. Maybe I could tease him later.

"I hope you'll let me watch." I took a sip of the wine. It was a rosé and actually pretty tasty.

Jack's head jerked up so fast, I was afraid he would have whiplash.

"What?"

I kept my face neutral. "I hope I can watch?"

His mouth gaped like he was a fish out of water. I was having a hard time not cracking up.

"You're alright that we're lovers?" His hands gripped the sides of the table.

Alright. Time to stop teasing the poor guy.

"Of course, I am. You've known each other longer than I've been alive. Besides, I have three mates. It's not like I can say anything. Why would I? You are both consenting adults. But, even if, for some stupid reason, that I wasn't okay with it, it's not up to me. It's your body." Leaning forward, I touched his right hand. "Besides, I think it's hot. So, can I watch?"

There was silence for almost a full minute. I had started to feel awkward. I'd just started to pull my hand away when he turned his over and laced our fingers together again.

"I want you to watch. I want you to be between us. I want to watch you ride me while sucking on Titus' cock. I want to be fucking you from behind while Billy takes your mouth and Titus fucks me."

Every word made my cheeks flush. By the time he

finished, I was pretty sure I could be mistaken for a maraschino cherry.

Well, alright then. Good to know we were on the same page.

I grabbed my napkin with my other hand and started fanning myself again.

"Holy shit." I couldn't look at him. I was going to combust right there.

"That's a yes?" Jack's voice was whispered, but I could hear the satisfaction in it.

I nodded. "Hell yes."

His chair slid out as he stood. He was at my side right after. I was on my feet, my arms going around his neck as his lips moved to meet mine.

Fireworks. Electricity. An ice storm. That's what his lips felt like as they moved across mine in a searing possession. His hands gripped my face as his tongue plundered inside to fight with mine.

When I sucked on his tongue, he growled so low, I could barely hear it, but, boy, did I feel it. My hands ran up under his shirt, my nails dragging along his skin. I wanted to mark him. Show the world he was mine. And Titus'. Perhaps Billy's one day.

"Come with me." Jack pulled back. His eyes were glowing white and I noticed that the snow around us had kicked up into a frenzy but didn't touch us in our little bubble.

"Here?" I was fluffy, but ice was still cold. I knew we'd break the table with how hard I wanted him to fuck me.

He chuckled, this time it sounded evil. I wanted him to do that more. It did things to me.

"No. I've had to clean up the ice when others have had

sex on it. It's a mess. Besides, I want you in a soft bed so the bruises you have are from my body. Not the ice."

I whimpered. Yup. I was a goner.

Jack waved his hand at the table and it just disappeared. I had to close my eyes and reopen them several times slowly to make sure I was seeing what I'd just seen.

"Wait. How?" Words were good.

"I'm the Winter King, *refr*." He said it like that would explain everything.

"Okay. You're going to have to explain it a little more." I placed my hands on my hips.

His sigh was annoyed. I pursed my lips about to say something bratty when he leaned down, swung me up over his left shoulder and started moving off the ice.

I squeaked. "Jack! Put me down!"

His answer was to squeeze my ass and his fingers dipped between the crack to rub at my pussy. Another squeak came out.

"My magic is the season. I am the season." He stepped out of the rink and began moving toward what I assumed was the small building he worked in and lived.

I assumed because I was hanging upside down. I slapped Jack's ass.

"I can walk!" I wiggled but he just squeezed my thigh.

"Yes, but I like you this way. Easy access." He laughed at his own joke and I shook my head, smiling.

Soon, we were inside and I was flipped over his shoulder onto a bed.

"Oof!" My grunt was cut off by Jack's lips. "Mmm!"

He didn't give me a chance to look around. Honestly, I didn't care.

Jack held himself above me as he kissed down along my shoulder. I pushed his shirt up, revealing his flat stomach.

"Sit up." Jack moved back, kneeling in front of me. "Take your clothes off."

My body moved at his command. My clothes were pushed to the floor before I could think. His gaze ignited my blood.

"Stop." He leaned forward, his hands cupping my breasts, rolling my nipples between his thumb and index fingers. "You're so beautiful."

My fingers ran through his hair. When he pinched my nipples, I tightened my fingers, pulling the strands tightly.

"Can we do the pleasantries and lovey stuff later? I was promised bruises."

Jack grinned. "Alright."

His hands gripped my waist and I was on my hands and knees.

"Oh!" Another squeak that turned into a moan as he slapped my ass before his palm rubbed the area.

The bed shifted behind me. I looked over my shoulder and moaned. Jack was naked. His cock was wide, it would stretch me out. My thighs quivered at the thought.

What caught my attention were his tattoos. One on each hip that flowed up his ribs. His tattoos were snowflakes with a flurry of snow that wound upward. Then I noticed his left nipple was pierced.

Holy smokes. Jack was smoking hot. I wanted to trace the tattoos with my tongue.

"Jack." I shook my ass. "Hurry up."

He did that evil chuckle again and my pussy was raring to go. His hand ran up my back as his other held his cock as he lined up behind me.

"You're so wet, baby." Jack's cock pressed into me slowly and I swear my eyes saw the inside of my brain.

As Jack moved inside of me, slowly, it was like a tornado

within my chest. The mate bond went crazy as it settled. That hadn't happened with the other two, but as soon as it solidified, Jack's hips moved in hard thrusts that I ended up having to clutch the sides of the bed because I started sliding forward.

The pain of our skins slapping together was an aphrodisiac. I'd be getting those bruises he promised. At least for a few hours until my shifting healing abilities healed them. His hand smacked my other ass cheek and my head fell forward onto the single pillow on the bed as little gasps fell from my lips.

With my ass up, my face down, I felt more vulnerable than I had in years. Yet, as he continued to fuck me senseless, I knew I was desired and wanted.

My pussy wanted his cock to stay inside as he began to pull out all of the way before slamming into his hilt in teasing strokes. With the heat of his chest and the feel of his skin, as he leaned over my back, I lost myself to one of the biggest orgasms I'd experienced. My scream was muffled in the pillow as his hands tightened around my hips and his speed picked up before he followed shortly after.

His weight shifted from my back and his body heat moved to my left side, next to the wall. His hands gentled as he pulled me half on his chest and he pushed the hair out of my eyes.

"Wow." We both spoke at the same time.

Wow was right.

CHAPTER 16

The next morning as I opened the shop, wearing the same clothes as yesterday with my hair a complete mess, I couldn't have been happier. I was sore along my ass, thighs, and backside. If I walked funny, it was a badge of honor.

Jack had kept me up all night, save a few blessed hours of sleep really early. He should be a bunny shifter with how fast he recovered for more rounds.

"What's got you humming this morning?" Frostine, a two tailed moon fox shifter I knew by proxy, had come in while I had been distracted.

I about jumped out of my skin and on top of the counter. Frostine stood in front with her hands in her front pockets. She had her hair up in a bun on the side of her head. That was kind of cool, actually. I didn't know her very well.

"Was I humming?" I pushed my hair out of my eyes, flustered. I turned around to grab a mug and started making a drink.

"Loudly and a little off key." Her smug tone was soft,

belaying that she wasn't being mean, just teasing. "Who's the lucky guy?"

I finished making her a hot chocolate that I named 'Malik's Delight' since I added a splash of vodka to it and served it in a see-through red cup. It might be morning, but who cared?

As I turned, pushed it across the counter to her, I couldn't help the grin.

"Jack Frost." I knew that he would be grumpy if random people started talking to him about us. So, it was perfect.

Frostine's eyes widened slightly as she blew on the hot chocolate. "Really? That cold hearted grumpy pants?"

I didn't like him being called cold hearted. He was far from it. But, he liked to appear that way. Hell, he'd been a jackass to me before Titus put his face into a table.

"He's actually quite passionate." I waved my hand in my face remembering how he'd held me up in his arms against the wall and screwed me into yet another happy ending.

"Obviously." Her sassy reply could have made paint dry. "Well, if he makes you happy, who am I to judge?" She shrugged as she sipped at Malik's Delight. "I wanted to come in to talk to you because early this morning, I noticed Samuel skulking around here, like he was looking for you. That guy gives me the creeps."

My good mood instantly dissipated. What had Samuel wanted? This guy seriously just wasn't giving up. I made the decision to confront him later today during a break and let him know that I wasn't folding to his demands. He was going to lose this war that he set out to win.

Frostine finished her drink. "Thank you for the hot cocoa. I'll see you later. Let me know if you need any help with this guy." She waved as she left.

I pulled out my phone and sent off a text to Billy.

Samuel was seen around my store again. I haven't seen him yet.

The three little dots appeared.

I'm getting tired of this guy. I'm coming over.

Well, that's not what I planned but hey. I'd get to see Billy. Worked for me. Maybe we could make out in the back. I hadn't christened the back room yet with sexy times besides that quick session with Titus.

The clock above the door chimed just as Billy walked into the shop. That was fast.

"Uh, how'd you get here so fast?" I met him around the counter and returned his kiss.

"I thought you might like a change of clothes so I was already on my way here." Billy handed me a bag. "I take it your date went well."

"You're my favorite." Hugging the bag to my chest, I had him bend so I could kiss his cheek.

"Damn right I am." Billy patted my ass as I went to the tiny restroom to change. "I'll watch the shop."

He'd packed my favorite lounge pants and one of his hoodies I stole. By the time I finished getting dressed, Billy had moved behind the counter and was handing a bag of popcorn to a couple of kids who'd come in.

I leaned against the wall and watched him. I was so lucky. I didn't know how it happened, but I was thankful that we were mates.

"So, I spoke with Titus." Billy gestured for me to sit at the counter. "Told him how you've wanted to go to his lodge for a long time. Does this weekend sound good?" He handed me a bag of popcorn.

Mmm. Buttery salty goodness.

"Popcorn is life." I took another handful. "I'm sure I could get Igor to watch the shop. Let's do it."

"I don't think we've had a vacation in awhile." Billy offered me the sweetest smile that made my heart skip a beat. "It will be nice, even if it's just one or two nights."

"You've not taken a break from your landscaping company since you started it three years ago." I finished the popcorn.

"Well, starting a business takes time and sweat. You're learning that." Billy moved to sit next to me.

"It hasn't been so hard." I bumped our shoulders. "It has actually been fun. After getting rid of my ex, the prank wars, and now Samuel? Other than that stuff it's been great."

I shuddered thinking about the chickens in my shop. Billy had been the one I'd called to come catch the little fuckers.

I was a red fox that was terrified of chickens. The irony of that was not lost on me.

When I was a little kid, I'd been exploring the woods near our house and roamed into our neighbors yard. I was used to helping out around the farm so I didn't think much of it. I'd been in my fox form when I ended up next to the chicken coop.

Me, being the smart and responsible child that I was, had decided to pop in to say hi to them since I was friends with them in my human form. I hadn't known that they wouldn't know it was me.

When I'd gone in, it was like the world had ended. Most of the fur on my tail and neck had been pecked away by the time I'd made it back outside.

I still couldn't see a live chicken without hyperventilating. I enjoyed eating them immensely in a sick revenge type of way.

"You're just getting the hard stuff done early. It'll be smooth sailing after." He scratched his beard. "I've been thinking about shaving and doing a goatee."

That was a change of subject.

"Um. Billy. You're an ironic enigma. You're a goat shifter named Billy. You eat grass for a living, and now you want a GOAT-ee?" My shoulders shook as I held back my laughter. "Really?"

His brows furrowed as he frowned. "Well, crap." His shoulders slumped in disappointment. "Guess I shouldn't."

"Honey," I swung my arm around his waist. "You want a goatee? Do it."

His arm went around my back. "You know it'll drive Maya nuts."

I giggled. "Now you have to do it. Annoying your sister is top priority."

CHAPTER 17

After Billy left, I decided that enough was enough. I'd give Samuel his answer and let him know that his playtime was over.

I put a break sign up at the store before I walked out. Ten minutes would do it. As I was walking toward Darcorp, I waved to Jack who was on the zamboni. He winked at me before flipping me off.

That was my mate.

My good mood helped my nerves as I pushed open the door into the nearly finished Darcorp building. The layout was similar to the larger stores around the rink. It seemed stale and, well, corporate.

Samuel was directing a pair of workers near the front of their counter. His hair was slicked back again, and as I got closer, my fox wrinkled her nose at the cologne he'd bathed in.

"Excuse me." I stopped about three feet from him. That was the closest that I was willing to be.

Samuel turned with a frown on his face. When he saw

that it was me, his frown turned into an alligator smile with all the teeth.

This guy was seriously creepy.

"Ah, Cider. Yes! Welcome! I hope you've come with good news." He clapped his hands together, rubbing them.

"Actually---"

He cut me off.

"Wait. wait! Before you give me your answer. Come with me!" He snapped his fingers, as if he were telling me to heel. I pressed my lips together to resist saying what I so wanted to. "I have something exciting to show you."

He walked into the kitchen, leaving me little choice but to follow him. He went over to one of the shiny new stoves. On it was a pot that was simmering with the ingredients next to it.

My little store had one stove in the back that I used to make everything and it was more than enough. This place had six. Talk about over kill.

Samuel stopped in front of the pot. He picked up the wooden spoon next to it and gave it a stir. The familiar scent had me stopping midstep. That scent. It was my secret hot cider!

I knew he'd somehow figured out the secret ingredient, but it had very specific instructions to actually make it. The ingredients had to be put in very specifically at different temperatures or it didn't come out just right.

That's why I hadn't had a total break down when I'd found that he'd somehow figured out the secret. I had memorized it a long time ago.

"How?" My mouth had gone dry.

Samuel glanced at me out of the corner of his eye, his smug look making anger bubble up within me.

"I can't divulge my secrets, of course. But, I thought it

would be a good idea to show this to you when you came to visit so that you could rethink your decision. Wouldn't it be a shame if you turned down our generous offer only to discover that your secret recipe really isn't all that secret?" He took a sip of the cider from the spoon. "Mmm. That is just delectable. I can see why it's so popular. The dash of chile really does just give it that kick, doesn't it?"

The floor fell away and I felt like I had fallen into a pit. How? How had he figured it out? I didn't even tell Billy about how to make it.

"How dare you?" My fist clenched. I was ready to give this guy the beating of a lifetime.

"I don't know what you mean." Samuel faced me. "But, I do hope this gives you more of a push to accept the offer. If you don't, we will go ahead with our new cider come opening day and you'll get nothing." He placed his hands in his pockets and rocked on his heels. "I'll give you the weekend to decide."

He ushered me out the kitchen, through the store, and out the door before I could think of what to say. I was standing in the middle of the path with people walking around me as I tried to figure out what had just happened.

My fox had started pacing. She was furious. I was furious. Yet, I'd just let him push me out without saying anything. I'd just turned to march back in there, consequences be damned, when Lys appeared in front of me.

"Hey, Cider." Her hands went to my shoulders. "What's wrong? You look like you're in shock."

I shook my head. "He knows my hot cider recipe. He knows how to make it. He doesn't just have the ingredients, he knows how to make it! I don't have that written anywhere and I've never told anyone how to!" Okay, there was the hysteria, I wondered when it would show up.

Lys face pinched. "There's got to be an explanation. Okay. Come on. Come to Triple E. I'll make you a cup of tea and we'll figure this out." She threaded her arm through mine and basically led me to her store on the other side of the rink.

Her shop was larger than mine. The decor was simple. Black and white. Her counter was on the side of the store. Her chairs were red leather.

She sat me at the counter and started moving around behind it.

"Is my brother happy?" I blurted out the question without thinking about it.

She froze in the middle of pouring the hot water from the kettle into one of her signature mugs.

"I like to think so. We're still learning about each other." She turned to me and handed me the cup with an herbal tea. It smelled divine. "The guys are all wonderful. We're even thinking about going on a trip together."

I sipped the tea. The tension lessened as I relaxed.

"This is good." Running my index finger around the edge. "You've been good for Quinten. We fight a lot but I love my brother. I just want him to be happy."

"He makes me happy. He's kind and funny." She got a starry eyed look.

Faking a gag, I rolled my eyes. "My brother is a lot of things, but funny is not one of them."

"He'd surprise you." She grabbed another cup. "So, I think it's safe to say that we need to get serious about this guy. Have you talked to Titus?"

"I mean, we talked about finding out about the whole stock issue." I looked down at the immaculate counter. "We just became mates. I don't want to be asking him for favors."

Lys filled her cup up with coffee. I hadn't known vampires could be affected by caffeine. Learn something new every day.

"If there's one thing that Titus enjoys, is taking care of the people he loves. Trust me. Took me nearly twenty-five years to get my independence." She poured a good amount of sugar into her drink. "Talk to him. Talk to all your mates now. You're all part of each other's lives now. I can guarantee that they're going to want to help you."

She had a point.

"Alright. I'll talk to them." I finished my tea. "I think this issue with Samuel might be personal. He's not going after any of the others as of yet. I need to find out why."

Lys took my cup and hers to a sink behind the counter. "Same. This guy is a sleaze ball. What if we spy on him?"

I ran my fingers through my hair. "Actually, that was one of my thoughts. Igor said she'd spy on him for me."

She blinked. "Igor? The talking Venus Flytrap?"

I grinned. "That's the one."

She laughed. "That's a brilliant idea. Let me know if I can help."

I stood. "Thank you, Lys." I paused in the doorway. "Really."

She nodded in response before I turned to leave. I walked back to my store. I pulled my phone out and called Billy.

"So," I bit my lip. "What do you think about asking Titus and Jack for help? With my situation?"

"I think it's a good idea." Billy yelled at one of his workers about moving a plant somewhere. "They might have different ideas that just the two of us wouldn't think of."

"I'll text them." I smiled as Billy cursed. It sounded like

he dropped something on his foot. "I'll see you after closing."

Hanging up, I sent a quick message to Igor, letting her know to go ahead with the plan before I pulled up a text message and attached both Jack and Titus to it.

I hate asking for help. It's just something I don't like to do but, I could use some help with the Samuel situation. He escalated it today.

Dots appeared almost instantly. Twenty bucks it was Titus.

Do I need to get rid of him? Yup. I'd been right.

No. No mysterious disappearances. Yet. Igor is going to spy on him for me. I'd like help figuring out what to do next, though.

Jack beat Titus to a reply.

I'll see what I can find myself, too. That guy is squirrely.

A chortle slipped out as I unlocked my store, flipped the open sign, and went behind the counter. Jack called him squirrely. I didn't know if that was cute or funny. Probably both.

I went in the back since there were no customers yet and started the familiar process of making my hot cider. I'd started making this drink years ago, before I'd graduated high school.

I'd always been a little weird. I mean, I am a fox shifter, but I was always bigger than other girls. That would sometimes mean that other kids weren't always so nice. They were only ever rude once, though.

They found their faces meeting my fist, or if Billy was around, his. But, it never failed that after that happened I went home and started making this drink. My grandpa had taught it to me when I was in the fourth grade and it had stuck with me.

When I'd made my tweaks to perfect it, that had felt like an accomplishment. I loved watching people take their first sip. The looks of shock, enjoyment, or pleasure always made me feel good. It was something that I had continued to make to get those looks.

Now some jackass was trying to take that away from me. I didn't know how he'd managed to figure it out. I'd find out and make him pay. My fox barked in agreement.

CHAPTER 18

"Cider!" Large arms encircled my waist from behind, swinging me around to look up into Titus' handsome face. His grin was all teeth as he held me to him. "You're off in your own little world. I tried to get your attention several times." His right hand cupped my face, running his thumb along my lower lip.

"Hi, Titus." I closed my eyes as I leaned my face into his palm. There was just something about that gesture that made me melt every time. "I'm sorry. I've just been trying to figure this whole situation out. I'm close to yanking my hair out. My fox is not happy with that at all."

My mind hadn't been able to shut off since two days ago. I'd gotten through the weekend rush. Now that it was the slowest day of the week, I just couldn't concentrate.

There was a little over two weeks left before Darcorp was ready for their opening deal that would tank my business, along with some of the others.

Igor had started watching Samuel. She hadn't found anything yet, but Igor was one being that I would never doubt. She'd find what she was looking for.

"I figured as much. Billy said you've been distracted." Titus pressed a kiss to my forehead sending those delicious tingles down my spine. "That's why I'm here. Besides missing you."

His arms were like steel around my waist. I wouldn't be able to wiggle out if I tried. Not that I planned to. Being surrounded by him was addicting. His smell, his touch. His taste. Oh, boy. I wanted to taste him again.

Wait. Behave. Middle of business day, Cider.

"So, you're here to distract me from being distracted?" I ran a finger along his collarbone and down his chest. "How are you going to do that?"

His other hand grabbed mine, stopping me from touching him. A rumble in his chest vibrated against my own. That was so hot.

"Cider, behave." Titus pressed a kiss to my palm. "I've arranged it so that you can take two days off. We're all going up to my lodge. Starting now."

I paused. "What? Really? Now? I don't have any clothes packed! Who is going to watch the store?"

"Taken care of." He leaned forward, brushing his nose up my neck. "Billy packed a few things for you. He's going to meet us at the lodge. Lys asked your brother to watch the store. Say yes."

I bit down on my lower lip. If Quinten was willing to watch the store, then I could go. I'd owe him a big favor. My fox bowed forward, her tail in the air. We wanted to play. Just a little.

"No."

Titus froze, his mouth near my ear. "No?"

"No." My chest became giddy. "I don't want to."

That was a downright lie.

Titus seemed to realize it, too. My tone must have

alerted him because it went up a little when I said I didn't want to.

His hands moved from my waist to my ass. I found myself lifted up, my legs wrapping around his hips. I clutched his shoulders. His hips molded to mine.

"I guess I'll just have to convince you." Titus' fangs flashed against the light, distracting me. "What shall I do?"

"Sex. Sex would be a good way to convince me." Yeah, I wasn't that great at playing keep-away. Not when it came to my mates. My body sang when they were near.

"I can do that." Titus moved, carrying me into the back room. "Stay." He sat me on the metal prep table against the wall. Good thing I'd cleaned it earlier this morning.

I squirmed but didn't move. Titus went back to the front. My ears twitched a little at the sound of the door locking. Good thinking.

I pulled my shirt off and was unhooking my bra when Titus came back into the room. His curse sent me into a spiral of giggles. He was in front of me in a blink, throwing my bra to the ground. His hands went to my legs, moving up to the waist of the pantline. I shifted as he pulled my leggings down, leaving them around my ankles.

"A thong? Are you trying to put me in the grave?" Titus moaned pushing my knees apart.

I was already wet. It seemed to be the constant when it came to my mates.

"I wanted to try them out." I shrugged. "See if you guys might like me wearing them."

"Baby, I dream of you wearing thongs and nothing else." Titus ran his thumbs along the inside of my knees.

My breathing picked up as he moved his hands upward.

"I am going to make you scream my name." Titus

kneeled in front of me, placed my legs over his shoulders and his tongue was on my clit.

Oh holy hot beverages. I clutched his hair. His tongue had to be illegal somewhere, I think I was beginning to make that a chant.

He flicked out his tongue along my pussy. Two of his fingers pressed inside of me, curling as he rocked them. Titus sped up his fingers as my legs tightened around his shoulders.

"Titus!" Whimpering, I wanted to fall back but I kept my fingers tight in his hair. "Don't stop!"

The pleasure built as he kept up a steadily increasing pace with his fingers, and his tongue. God, that tongue.

Then I felt something that rocked my world, exploding my pleasure in a cascading effect. One of his fangs brushed along my clit as he sucked it into his mouth. The jolt of pain with the pleasure made me scream.

My legs shook as I came so hard, the world went black for several seconds. Titus stood, leaning over me as he licked his lips. The glint in his eyes made me shiver.

"Delicious." His purr was soft as he kissed my shoulder. "Your taste is just as addicting as your hot cider."

"Titus, I didn't get naked just so you could eat me out, you know that, right?" My breathy reply wasn't as snarky as I had meant it to be.

"Oh, baby girl." His hands curled around my hips, pulling me to the edge of the table. "I know." His hands left my skin.

I watched as he pushed his pants down, his cock hard as it bobbed. My tongue ran along my top lip. Cocks shouldn't be beautiful, but his was.

Titus' hands gripped my hips again. His lips met mine as he pressed inside of me. My whimper was muffled as our tongues began to dance with each other. His cock stretched my walls. My back arched on its own accord.

"Titus, please!" I clutched his back, my nails digging into his skin. "Bite me!"

He went motionless. "Baby girl, are you sure? You'll be a bit woozy in the car."

"I'm begging." I wrapped my legs around him. "Please."

That growl, sounding demonic this time, came from out of him again. His thrust inside of me made me cry out. His lips moved along my jawline, down to the right side of my neck. There was a sting as his teeth sank into my skin. It didn't last long before the force of his sucking pulled my blood into his mouth.

I was sinking in euphoria. Every thrust was followed by a pull from his mouth. I knew I was going to come again as he picked up his speed. My fingers moved up his back to his hair. I couldn't think.

"Titus!" My scream was muffled by his hand as he hurriedly covered it.

"Cider." His mouth pulled away from my neck, his tongue licking the open wounds from his fangs. My shifter healing ability is already closing them. "You're mine."

Titus' cock pistoned, his hips slamming against mine. The table rocked with each thrust. He grunted as I cried out as I came around his cock, my hips jerking upward. That sent him over the edge with me.

"Shit." His hands rested on the side of my shoulders as we both gasped for air.

"I'm convinced. Let's go."

He threw his head back and laughed.

CHAPTER 19

"Why am I not surprised that you drive a super fancy car?" I ran my fingers along the supple brown leather seat.

"I enjoy the finer things at this stage of my life." Titus drove like he did everything else in his life. With cocky confidence and purpose.

We were headed further into the mountains out of town. We'd locked up after closing, dropped my car off at the house, and headed out. I'd eaten a little bit of popcorn before we'd left so I'd make the trip without getting hangry.

"You talk like you're an old man." I winked at him as he looked at me out of the corner of his eye with a smirk on his lips. "One would think that you were as old as Jesus instead of just the Romans of old."

His eyes comically widened. "Now, that is just cruel, baby girl."

We turned right onto a paved road with a large sign welcoming visitors.

"You should talk to Jack about how old he is." Titus reached out with his right hand to hold my left.

"Oh, I can only imagine. Especially if he is the 'Winter King'." I kissed his knuckles.

"If you start doing that, baby girl, be ready for the consequences." His hand tightened on mine, making me grin. I liked the reactions I could get out of him.

"Oh, fine." I put our hands in my lap. "I'll behave." Sike. I promptly pulled his hand up and sucked on his middle finger.

"Cider!" The car swerved as Titus lost control of it momentarily as I cackled gleefully.

"You'll pay for that, my dear." He took his hand away from mine and firmly locked it on the steering wheel. "Mark my words."

The scenery outside changed as we got closer to the big building that had come into view. My mouth popped open a little.

"Lodge? That's not a lodge. That's a fucking CASTLE, Titus!" I glared at him. "How in the world did you get a castle out here?"

His shoulders shook in silent laughter as he pulled the car to the front doors where a valet stood behind a small wooden podium. Titus parked and was out the door and at mine before I could finish unbuckling.

"Well, I built it. That's how it got here." I narrowed my eyes at his arrogant remark that just rolled off his tongue so easily.

I took his offered hand as he helped me out of the sleek car and handed the keys to a young looking troll.

"Thanks, Teddy." Titus nodded at him as he smoothly moved my hand to the crook of his arm. "There aren't any humans here, so you can relax as much as you like."

The large wooden doors opened automatically. Heat hit me in the face as we stepped inside. The decor was old school. Wooden beams across the ceiling, the walls were stone with the heads of animals scattered about.

I wasn't sure I liked that part of the place and said so.

"Dead animals are so drab."

Titus pulled me to one of the walls where a large wolf head howled. "Look closer."

Leaning forward, I stood on my toes to get a better look. I didn't know what I was looking at. I'd just opened my mouth to say so when the wolf head just blinked out of existence and in its place was a bear in the middle of a large snarl.

I stumbled back, tripping over my own feet. Titus caught me under my arms, keeping me from falling. His chuckle was low in my ear.

"Holograms. Nifty aren't they? The theme for the winter is old rustic lodge. When spring rolls around, I'll probably have them change it to flowers or something." He looked down at me with a free expression, melting my insides.

I fell in love in that instant. His face was open for the first time, like he'd finally relaxed and was in his comfort zone. He was my mate but I hadn't thought of those kinds of feelings yet. I hadn't thought we were at that stage.

Guess my heart proved me wrong.

"Titus." A man's voice from across the room distracted us.

I stopped moving for a brief second. This guy had even redder hair than I did. Strands of his hair were standing up, making him look wild. With the way he had his hand on his hip, the curl of his lips, he oozed cockiness.

"That wine you suggested was fantastic. You're not half bad for a vampire. I can't wait to rub it in my brother's face that a vampire with the same name is smarter than he is with great business sense, unlike him." He slapped Titus' shoulder as he grinned wickedly. "Granted, calling you by his name is still weird. I still expect to see him when I hear it."

"Titus isn't that rare of a name." Titus' left eye looked like it had a twitch, it seemed this wasn't the first time he'd been compared to the guy's brother.

Whoever this guy was, I liked him. He had my mate in a tizzy and that was hilarious.

The guy just waved off Titus' comment. "Not where I come from." He glanced at me, offered an extravagant bow with hand flourishes. "I am Lance. It is my pleasure to meet you."

He took my hand and kissed it, all the while looking at Titus from the corner of his wicked eyes. He was enjoying ruffling Titus' feathers. I could only imagine how he acted with his actual brother.

"Nice to meet you, too." It wasn't my fault that I was blushing crazily. The guy was wickedly sinful.

"I'll catch up with you later, Titus." As Lance walked off, I leaned against the bar. Oh, man. I had to fan my cheeks.

"You're pretty impressive for an old man, you know that?" I offered a soft smile, trying to distract Titus.

Titus looked up from the paperwork he'd been looking at on the other side of the desk. "Am I?" He leaned forward.

Tilting my head, I looked out over the open lounge area. "A place safe for supernaturals to come and just relax? Even Silver Springs has humans. We can't be ourselves even there all the time." I gestured to a young male angel on the arm of an older man that my fox thought was some kind of spell caster that involved blood. "Where else could these people go in this area that would be safe to do so?"

"I wanted a place for my family. It just evolved from there." Titus shrugged as he handed the paperwork he'd been going over to the worker he'd taken over for while speaking with Lance. "Now," he grinned at me. "Want to go see where we're staying?"

Jumping forward, I spun with my hands on my hips. "Lead on, sir!" I saluted him before I cracked up as he rolled his eyes at me.

"You're not as funny as you think you are." His hand rested on the middle of my back as he led me toward the elevators on the other side of the room.

"Darling," we stepped into the open elevator and he pressed the penthouse floor, "I am the funniest person you'll ever meet."

Titus pushed me against the wall and his lips covered mine. Apparently, he wanted to shut me up. I was so okay with that.

His tongue took over my mouth, making my knees weaken. The way he curled it left me a moaning mess. My moans just encouraged him to deepen the kiss as he held the back of my head with one hand while the other pressed against the wall next to my shoulder. I clutched the front of his shirt.

The ding announcing that we'd arrived at our floor pulled us apart by a few inches. His eyes had darkened, his pupils wide.

"Really?" Billy's tone was dry. "The elevator?"

Titus moved, letting me see Billy, who stood in front of the elevator, his foot keeping the door open. His beard was twitching at the corners of his mouth as he fought to keep a serious face.

"You're just jealous Titus got to do it first." I flung myself into his arms, jumping up on instinct. Billy easily caught me, gripping my legs around his waist.

"Damn right." He kissed me roughly, claiming his own mark on me. My body molded against him.

A hard body pressed from behind me. Titus' hands ran up my back. I could feel his breath on the back of my neck and I shivered.

"Maybe moving into the room might be a good idea. Unless you feel like giving those cameras in the hallway a show." Jack saved us from embarrassing ourselves. He was leaning against the only door on the floor a few feet away.

Titus gave a sigh that sounded like he was suffering. I snickered as I held onto Billy's shoulders as we followed Jack into the room.

"Woah." The room was completely different from down stairs. The contemporary style was very Titus. Silver was the prominent color scheme. The open floor plan was beautifully designed. There were stairs down into the living room. The far wall was just windows overlooking part of the woods and part of the vineyard.

There was a curved couch in the middle of the room. Billy sat down in the middle of it with me in his lap.

"Place is ritzy, right?" He stroked my back as I glanced around. I almost purred.

"Is this where you live, Titus?" I watched Jack sit at one of the stools at the bar that was in the kitchen.

"Yes. It's my little nest." Titus moved behind the bar. He poured what looked like whiskey into a glass and handed it to Jack.

The scruff of Billy's beard against my neck made me want to mew like a cat. His lips moved along my skin. I pressed further into his body, my nipples hard. His hands were roaming along my limbs, setting my blood on fire.

"So, starting right away it seems?" Jack tipped the glass back as he downed the whiskey.

"It would seem so." Titus unbuttoned his cuffs, rolling up his sleeves. "Billy, if you pause for a moment?"

Billy groaned, his hands tightened on my thighs. "Why?" His hardened state under me made me wiggle to mess with him.

"Alright, Jack. Same rules apply. No dismemberment. Please, try not to break anything too expensive." Titus moved a crystal vase from the counter next to him into a cabinet.

What was he talking about? I looked at Billy but he shrugged.

"No dick shots or hits that cause unconsciousness." Jack handed his empty glass to Titus who placed it in the sink.

"Guys?" I raised a hand. "What's going on?"

"You see, Cider," Jack stood, unbuttoning his shirt halfway. "Titus and I have a history. But we're both tops."

If it was possible, Billy had gotten even harder. His hands dug into my sides.

"You two fight for top." His rasp was low.

"That we do." Titus picked up a bottle on the bar and tossed it to Billy, who caught it without even blinking. "Hold on to that until we need it, will you?"

Oh, that was hot. I watched with wide eyes. Jack moved away from the bar as Titus moved slowly around the counter.

A blur and Titus was no longer there. The slap of a fist meeting muscle. The grunt of Titus. A blur of black clothing.

The two were fighting, yet they were moving so fast, I could barely see what was happening.

Then there was a crash as Jack was thrown into the wall near the door. He grunted as he fell to a knee. His lip was bleeding but he was grinning like a madman.

"Are you angry at me, Titus?" His taunt was flung out as he side stepped another blur, swinging out with his fist.

Titus ended up on the ground rubbing his jaw.

"Of course I'm angry at you." He stood, brushing his pant legs. "You were unnecessarily rude to our mate. You hurt her." The last part was hissed as Titus' lip lifted to show his fangs.

Jack cracked his neck, rolling his shoulders and his fingers sparked with magic. "I did."

They blurred again. Billy winced with me as we listened to the sound of them hitting each other. Billy was still hard, he rubbed his palm over my pussy. My leggings were already soaked through.

"Your scent." His soft growl seemed to echo in the room over the fighting. "I want to drown in it."

A crash happened in front of us. Jack had been thrown into the coffee table, breaking it. He groaned in pain as he rolled to his side. He attempted to stand but Titus was there, kicking him to the floor. Titus pressed his foot to Jack's neck.

"Yield." His accent had thickened.

"Bite me," Jack choked out as he punched Titus in the leg.

Why was this so hot?

Another blur and Jack was thrown into the coach on his stomach with Titus pressing him into the cushions.

"Gladly." His hiss was loud as Titus bit into Jack's neck roughly, jerking his hair backward.

A glance down and both were hard and straining against the cloth.

So that was why it was so hot. They were turned on by the violence they were doing against each other.

Billy shifted me so that I faced Jack and Titus and his hand went inside the front of my pants, his middle finger rubbing at my clit.

"Oh!" My hips bucked. My clit was sensitive from earlier. My legs trembled as Billy began to slowly move his finger in a circle, torturing me.

"Give up!" Titus' command brought my attention back to them as Billy continued to torture me.

Blood from the bite mark stained Jack's shirt. He drove his elbows back into Titus' stomach but it didn't seem to phase Titus. He grinned as he licked at the trickling blood.

"I'm going to fuck you so hard that your legs won't work for the rest of the day," Titus whispered loudly enough that Billy and I could hear. I shivered and my hands clutched Billy's arm.

Jack bucked underneath Titus, which just made it easier for Titus to thrust his hips against Jack's ass, grinding against him.

Jack let out a moan even as he struggled against the hold that my vampire mate had on him. He didn't use his magic. Titus yanked Jack's hands above his head, held them there with one of his and he ripped Jack's pants off. The sound of cloth ripping had Billy's finger on my clit picking up its pace.

My toes curled. "Oh!"

"Billy, the bottle, please." Titus didn't look at us, his full attention on Jack. The muscles in his arm clenched as Jack yanked, trying to dislodge his hold.

Billy handed the bottle over to Titus with his free hand.

The top of the bottle flew across the room as Titus upended the contents onto Jack's skin.

Lube. The bottle was lube. Oh boy. It was going to happen. I shifted in Billy's lap, which made him flick my clit, his other hand moved to press against my stomach.

"Fuck!" Jack cursed loudly as we watched Titus press a finger inside of him.

"You're so tight." Titus' hand twisted. "Relax. Let me make you feel so good." His rumble turned all of us on by the twitching of Billy's cock and the breath of air that Jack sucked in.

My head fell backward onto Billy's shoulder as his finger brought me to climax. "Billy!" My head turned into his neck and I bit down as I rode the high from it.

The slap of skin distracted me. Billy and I looked at Titus and Jack again.

Titus had removed his finger from Jack and smacked his hand down on Jack's ass. I was just in time to watch as Titus pushed into Jack.

Both grunted. Titus' hands moved to Jack's back, sliding down with his nails dragging the shirt. Jack pushed himself up onto his hands, they were curled around the cushion.

"Cid." Billy's hot breath against my ear had me raring to go. "Stand up for a second."

I scrambled out of his lap as he pushed his hips up to remove his pants and boxers. Then I was back in his lap with mine gone and I couldn't remember how that had happened. His cock slid inside of me as if we'd done this a million times. Pleasure shot through me.

"Harder, you asshole! You promised me rough!" Jack's hiss was full of anger. "Fuck me!"

That's when Titus seemed to let go. He wasn't the tender lover I'd been with. He turned feral.

His lip pulled back, eyes wild as he let loose and fucked Jack. Their grunts and moans just spurned to turn me on even more.

Billy too. His thrusts inside of me became erratic the longer we watched Titus and Jack.

When Titus shoved Jack's face into the cushions and leaned over him as he slammed into him, I trembled. The couch moved a little with every thrust. Titus bit down on Jack's shoulder, taking deep pulls of blood.

As I remembered how delicious that had been, I came around Billy's cock again, whimpering.

I wanted more. No, needed.

Billy dug his fingers into my skin as he shuddered underneath me. His last jerk had me squeaking as he came inside of me.

He held me to his chest as we continued to watch Titus ravage Jack. He'd bitten Jack in several spots at this point.

"Titus!" Jack threw his head back and his legs gave out as he came.

Titus was coming on the edge of Jack's orgasm. He collapsed on top of Jack, both out of breath.

"I call next." Billy held his hand up.

Laughter filled the room.

CHAPTER 20

Room service was ordered. I was in Heaven. The wine was sweet and tart.

"Titus, if this wasn't so far from the store, I'd move in just for this perk." I cut into the salmon, taking a big bite.

Titus was lounging on the couch, his right leg over the top. He'd gotten plenty of blood from Jack, apparently, and didn't need or want any solid food. That meant more for me.

"Is that how I get into your heart? The saying is through your stomach, isn't it?" He was so relaxed that his foot that was in the air moved to a silent beat. He was on a blood high.

I giggled. He was really cute. I glanced at Jack, who was eating his second steak. He looked tired but satisfied. His hair was disheveled. He'd changed into new clothes.

Billy finished his eggplant parmesan and patted his stomach.

"Man. Sex, a show, good food and drink? I am fat and happy tonight." He stretched with his arms over his head. He only had shorts on.

I snickered into my wine glass as I watched Jack run his eyes down Billy's chest. Well. Looked like Billy was probably going to be bottom to both of my other mates. I couldn't wait.

"Is anyone up for a nap?" Titus lifted his head, blinking owlishly.

"That sounds good to me." Billy stood, walked over to the couch, and fell onto it. Half his body covered Titus', who grunted at his weight. "Ah, yes. This is the spot."

Jack finished his steak, setting his knife and fork down. He looked at me. "Would you like to go for a walk in the woods? Maybe shift and we can play in the snow?"

My fox perked up at the same time I did. That sounded like fun.

"Hell yeah." I hopped off the bar stool. "I'd love to shift and play."

Jack started piling the dirty dishes on the tray that they'd been delivered on.

"Sounds good to me." He offered a small smile at me. "I haven't played in the snow for a long time."

Some alone time with Jack? Yes, please. I shifted without taking clothes off. By the time I crawled out from under my shirt, Jack was by the door waiting for me.

"Have fun!" Titus' voice was muffled where he'd buried his face in the crook of Billy's neck. Billy was already snoring.

As we rode down in the elevator, I batted at Jack's leg. My fox widened her eyes as we stared up at him. Our tail moved slowly back and forth.

"Yeah?" He squatted next to me, his fingers scratching behind my ear.

Oh. Ooh. That was the good stuff! Scritches behind the ear were closest to sex you could get to.

Jack laughed softly. "Can I carry you out?" He held out his arms.

I hopped up into them and curled my tail. My fox was purring up a storm.

The lobby was filled with people. Good thing he was holding me. Dodging that many feet would have been fun, but distracting. We passed the lounge area where I could see Lance drinking from a tumbler and staring out one of the many windows.

Instead of heading to the entrance, Jack moved toward the back of the room where another large doorway opened up to a patio area that overlooked the extensive vineyard.

It was cooler up on the mountain. My fur kept me toasty. Jack, being the Winter King, didn't seem to be bothered in the t-shirt and jeans he was in, either.

His long legs took us into the wooded area. The tree branches were heavy with snow. I couldn't wait to play in the snow drifts.

I was impatient. Starting to wiggle in Jack's arms, I pushed off his chest with my paws and took off into the wood with Jack's laughter following me.

Happiness filled me as we flew through the foliage. A blast of cool wind pushed me over, and I went tumbling with a squeak.

"You're it." Jack bent over me, his hair brushing my whiskers. "Can you keep up, little fox?" His pupils turned white as wind picked up around him, lifting him a few inches off the ground.

Oh. He could fly because of the wind?

I flipped onto my paws and yipped, my tail going crazy. Let's do this!

Jack turned, flying off with me right behind. Snow flew

around us in flurries as we played tag for what felt like minutes but actually ended up being a few hours.

It was nice being able to just let go and have fun. My worries and stress just melted away. Jack even laughed when I'd manage to jump on him to tag him.

At one point, I'd managed to hide high in a tree from him. He'd looked around for me, calling my name. When he'd faced away from me, I jumped onto his head, clinging to him.

His loud shout followed by his laugh startled some birds nearby. He lifted me off of him, flipped me on my back, and held me like a child. I snapped at his fingers a few times before he started to rub my belly.

My fox caved in a crescendo of purrs. She was a hussy. I was, too.

"I've been around since the dark ages." Jack sat down at the bottom of the tree, the snow cradling him as he continued to pet me. "I've seen the horrors that this world has to offer. Humans being the worst."

I watched his expression. He looked haunted. My tail flicked along his cheek, bringing his attention down to me.

His lips softened, curling up. "I know I'm not nice. I don't want to be. Titus is one of the few beings in this world that I get along with on occasions. Then you just appear in front of me. All curves, sass, and laughter. My heart's desire. I panicked." His index finger scratched just behind my ear. "What I said to you, both times, was cruel, and for that, I'll be trying to make up for it for the rest of our lives, if you'll keep me close."

I licked his palm. He'd more than made up for his assholish ways. I could feel his sincerity.

Jack glanced up at the sky. "It's starting to get late. Why don't we head back? We can get the other two up and we can roast marshmallows at one of the fire pits outside on the patio."

I yipped excited at the prospect but I let him hold me the way back to the room. I was comfortable and content to stay exactly where I was.

I'd be okay with my mates, no matter what came my way. I knew that now.

CHAPTER 21

The two days off seemed to fly by. I spent it mostly naked with my mates. The sex was hot. It was great. We cuddled, we laughed, we played video games.

Turns out, Titus could kick both Billy's and my ass at most of the video games we all played. Jack refused to play. He said it was because technology bugged the shit out of him, but I think he just didn't want to admit that he'd never actually played before.

I'd gotten a few updates from Igor. She'd been following Samuel since I'd sent her the text with the go ahead. She said that he was a disgusting human. His eating habits reminded her of a starving rabid racoon.

The only thing that she'd noticed that was out of the ordinary, was that he seemed to be able to answer questions before they'd even be asked. Every time.

I'd agreed with her that it was suspicious. For all that we knew, Samuel presented himself as human. He was certainly as greedy as a human. His uncanny creepiness aside, there was nothing outstanding about him. There was no obvious giveaway that he was anything but a standard human.

Quinten had texted me a few times. The delivery of supplies from Titus' guy had arrived. It came at the right time. Quinten said he was down to just one gallon of my cider. I'd be making a ton when I opened the store the next day. Good thing Igor was going to come by to help in the front while I worked in the back.

"Why don't you just come to our house for a few days?" Billy had his head in Titus' lap. He'd already packed up his things last night. "You said this place practically runs itself, right?"

I watched as Titus offered a comforting smile to Billy. "I did say that." He played with a stand of Billy's hair. "I accept your invitation."

My stomach fluttered. I squeezed Jack's hand. "You're coming, too. You can commute to work with me."

Jack was flipping through his phone without his other hand. "I thought that was a given."

"Good." I pushed our shoulders together, laying my head on his chest. "It's alright that you're grumpy, you know? We don't care."

He set his phone down before stroking my hair. "I'll get better with you. Probably Billy. Not Titus. Titus is a dick."

I choked on my laugh as they both simultaneously flipped each other off. I think that meant future fights for dominance and I was here for it.

My phone rang. I didn't recognize the number so I let it go to voicemail. Not more than five minutes later, the same number called again. This time I answered.

"Hello?" I sat up, away from Jack but kept our hands together.

"Hey, it's Igor."

I looked at the number that had called. "Igor? This isn't your cell phone."

"No," Igor yawned. "It died on me. This is an old pay phone. Can't believe it actually works. I've only seen them in old movies."

"That's interesting? Igor, what's up?" If I didn't get her to focus, she'd keep rambling. Jack raised a brow at me but I shook my head at him.

"I think I found out how Samuel got your secret recipe." Igor started whispering into the phone, like she wasn't alone. "When will you be back at the shop?"

"You found out? That's great! We'll leave now! I'll call Quinten and he can have Lys meet us in the shop. See you soon?" I hung up and stood. "Guys! We need to go! That was Igor. She thinks she figured out how Samuel messed with my cider!"

Billy sat up as Titus leaned forward.

"That's great, Cid!" Billy grabbed me around the waist and pulled me into his lap as I laughed. "Sounds like we need to get back."

"I know we weren't going to leave for a few more hours, but it's important." I glanced at the three of them. "I'll make it up to you."

"Cid, of course, we'll go. This is important to you. A few hours isn't such a big deal." Billy ruffled my hair. "Dork."

"Let's get going. We can take my car." Titus stood, offering to help me up but Billy stood with me.

"That sounds better than taking the bus again." Billy set me down to grab our bags near the door. Jack was already at the elevator waiting for us.

Giddiness made me jump up and down a little in impatience. For the first time since Samuel showed up at my doorstep, there was hope for my store.

CHAPTER 22

By the time we got back to the rink, I was basically vibrating out of my own skin. Titus hadn't even turned off the car and I was out running out of it to my shop.

Igor was sitting at the table closest to the counter while Lys sat on one of the stools. Quinten was behind it, leaning over to speak with his mate. They all looked up as I came in, followed shortly after by my own mates.

"Oh, look, you have your own harem." Igor had a shot of vodka in front of her. "Good job. They look strong." I think it might not have been her first.

I glanced at my brother. "Uh. Is she drunk?"

He shrugged sheepishly. "She already downed a whole bottle."

Oh boy.

I sat across from her, taking her hand. "Igor?" She hadn't sounded drunk on the phone. "You alright?"

Her eyes looked glassy. Oh yeah. She was wasted. Iris was going to kill me.

"Samuel can read minds. That's what I figured out."

She held her hand to her mouth when a hiccup slipped out. "I had Lawrence's help. We went to talk to him. Asked about employment. The guy just looked at us, stared right at Lawrence."

She went to grab the shot glass but I pushed it out of her reach. "Sweetie, I think you've had enough. Tell me what happened."

Igor sighed, running a hand through her bouncy curls.

"He laughed. Said that he knew we were just spying for you. Then he looked at Lawrence and said, 'You don't love her. Just tell her already. You're not some pawn in her life.' After that, Samuel laughed again, told me to stop trying to run it through in my head, that looking into it was giving him a headache and went into the back room." She laid her head on the table, turning her cheek to look up at me mournfully. "Lawrence doesn't love me. Why?"

"Oh, hunny." I took her hand. "Did Lawrence say anything?"

I'd go over what she'd discovered about Samuel later. Right now, my friend needed help.

Her hiccups started coming faster. "No." Hic. "He just looked at me with his big, sad eyes. Like I'd disappointed him. Again." Hic. Tears slid down her face. "Why can't I figure this out? I don't like being human. I should just stay a plant."

Quinten rounded the counter, took Lys hand, and left through the front door. Titus followed with Billy and Jack to give Igor some privacy.

"Igor." I lifted her chin up gently to make sure she was looking at me. "Hey. This is all new to you. You're trying. That means a lot. Lawrence sounds like he has his own internal struggles that he just isn't sharing. Do you really want to be with a," I paused. I wasn't quite sure what to call him, "male who isn't willing to at least try like you've been?"

She blinked owlishly, but her glassy eyed stare started to clear. "You know. You're right. I've been trying really hard to understand all of these emotions. For Lawrence. Yet, he's not tried once to see why I want to be this way." Her back straightened and she grabbed the shot glass from across the table, chugging it. "I'm a catch! I'm motherfucking Igor! I don't need a male to have self-worth!" She slammed the glass down. "Thanks, Cider. I needed that kick in the ass." She wiped her mouth. "Let's get down to business. You can bring back the others. I'm good now."

I made a mental note to make sure to talk to Iris later on. Just to give her a heads up. She might be able to hide Lawrence from Igor's wrath. Poor guy. He messed with the wrong lady.

The others came back into the store when I caught Quinten's eye from outside. I settled more into my chair as I looked at Igor.

"So, he's a mind reader." I tapped my fingers on the table. "I wasn't aware of any kind of supe that had that power, unless it was some kind of spell."

Hands pressed into the muscles on my shoulders, kneading them gently. I looked up and offered Jack a soft smile in thanks. His beautiful clear eyes relaxed me.

"What if he is human? There are humans with some powers, albeit rare." Lys stood next to Quinten, or rather, was leaning against him. "Like those psychics. Maybe he's like that?"

"He's had a witch in his bloodline." Titus started to make some hot chocolate. "So, you're half right and half wrong. He possesses a tiny bit of magic that's generated in this power. It also means that I can take care of him without bothering with the human authorities." He offered us an evil look that had me crossing my legs under the table. "It was one of the things I'd found out about him, but it hadn't seemed to be important until now because he didn't present as supernatural."

It was the fangs. It had to be the fangs. That man was so hot it was just not fair.

Jack's hands squeezed my shoulders, bringing my attention back to the situation at hand.

"Titus," I blew him a kiss. "As much as I appreciate the thought of you destroying him for me, I think we should confront him and give him the option to leave town with Darcorp, or we let you have fun with him with Igor. She did find out about him for us. It only seems fair." I looked at Lys. "Does that sound good to you?"

The vampire woman tapped a finger on her lips as she thought.

"It would probably be better to avoid all out murder at the rink, Titus. I think if we can get this asshole and that sad excuse of a company out of here before they can damage the other stores." She patted Quinten on the arm. "Your brother was ready to go rip his face off this morning." She glanced at me. "It was adorable."

My cheeks hurt as I grinned at him. "Really? You were being over protective brother mode?"

Quinten just rolled his eyes. "Did you have to tell her that?"

"Yup," Lys popped.

"Alright, back to the matter at hand." Jack ran his fingers through my hair. It felt so good. "Are we really just going to go up to him?"

"No." I paused to make sure they were paying attention. "I'm supposed to meet with him and give him my answer.

That should be it. I'll tell him that if he doesn't leave town, I'll expose him with everyone's help and he'll never be trusted by any supe in the community. And, let's be honest, some of the less savory people won't like having a mind reader around town. They'd take care of him for us." Aka Igor.

Billy pulled out the chair next to mine and sat down. "I don't want you alone when you meet with him."

Warmth spread through me. I loved him. My big mountain goat.

"I won't be. You and the others will be in the back." I traced his knuckles with my fingers. "I'm sure I won't be in any danger." My fox snorted. She'd tear the man's jugular out with her teeth given the chance but, if being all protective made my mates feel good, I'd let them think I'd need it.

"When should we do this?" Jack still stood behind me, offering his support.

"He said I'd only have the weekend to think about my answer to him. So, probably tomorrow. I'll leave a note for him at Darcorp to meet me here after closing?" I glanced around the shop and the others all nodded. "Alright. We have a plan."

CHAPTER 23

Time seemed to slow down over the next twenty-four hours. My mates and I went back to Billy's and my place to relax until the next day. We talked in length about how I would prevent Samuel from reading my mind when I confronted him.

Jack was the one who knew how to do it.

"When he's in front of you, imagine something around you. Most people visualize a wall, they build it up brick by brick. The few times I've had to shield my mind, I used my ice as my wall." He pressed his index finger to the middle of my head. "What you use will be up to you, but whatever you do choose, you should start practicing through the night and during the day tomorrow so you're prepared. I doubt he's strong enough to get through it."

I tried thinking about a wall. It was uncomfortable and didn't feel right. My fox nudged me when I looked out the window. I could visualize the woods. Trees.

Thinking of a wall of trees came easier for me. The woods were where I was the most comfortable. My fox preened that she'd been the one to figure it out.

Titus started to teach me to play chess while I worked on keeping the wall of my mind always in the forefront. I wasn't very good. I just wanted to bash the opponents pieces to smithereens. Apparently, that wasn't the kind of play that chess required. I lost count how many times I lost.

Billy, on the other hand, was a natural. He and Titus played long into the night while I went to bed. Jack joined me and we had a little bit of naughty time before we both passed out in a blissful sleep.

When my alarm went off in the morning, I didn't want to move. My mates were surrounding me on the bed, all of them somehow touching me. The only reason, besides the thought of showing Samuel up, that I got out of bed was because I had been about to pee myself. That would have been wholly unattractive.

Climbing over the body limbs of hot men was a great way to start the day. I was low-key nervous about the meeting with Samuel but only because I didn't want him to give anyone my recipe. It wasn't like it was super secret. Someone could probably figure it out, but the point was that it was mine. This was a great way to get rid of our problems, though. If he left town, he couldn't hurt anyone else.

The shower was on full blast, the hot water running over my breasts when arms went around my waist. I leaned back against Billy, looking up at him. He was still waking up but his cock was at full attention. He'd opened the bathroom door so quietly and I'd been so preoccupied I hadn't heard.

"Hey, goatface." I stood on my toes to kiss just under his chin. "Can I tell you something?"

He nuzzled my neck, his beard scratching my skin softly. "What's that?"

"I love you."

He froze, his hands on my stomach. "Cid?"

"You heard me." I tilted my head forward, getting my hair wet.

Billy turned me, keeping me from slipping, and his lips crashed into mine. His teeth bit down on my lower lip, sucking on it.

I whimpered as I clutched his forearms. He didn't let me up for air until I almost passed out. He'd just about kissed me unconscious. His arms were the only thing keeping me upright.

"I love you, too." His voice was raspy with emotion. "I can't believe how fast I've fallen for you, but I have."

I ran my hand along his jaw. "Billy," I paused when the bathroom door opened again. Titus leaned against the doorframe.

"Now this is a beautiful sight to wake up to." His arms were crossed over his chest in a tantalizing view. "As much as I would like to continue watching, Cider, you're going to be late for work, are you not?"

I blinked. "My alarm just went off. I should still have an hour or so."

"That was your third alarm." His amusement was palpable. He laughed as I cursed loudly.

"One of these days I'll not have to scramble!" Shampoo and conditioner took an extra few minutes while Billy stepped out of the shower to give me the space I needed.

"I'll believe it when I see it." Billy chuckled as he wrapped a towel around his waist. "I'll make a quick breakfast." He pushed Titus out of the doorway and they left me to the rest of my shower.

Jack was still asleep when I came out of the shower. He looked peaceful. I didn't want to wake him.

Yet, if I had to work, so did he.

With a quick jump, I pounced on top of him. "Wake up, sleeping beauty!" My hands bounced on his chest a few times as he grunted.

"Ah!" He sputtered. "Cider!" He groaned, rubbing his head. "Why?"

"We have to go to work." With a roll, I was off the bed and searching for something to wear. "No sleep for you!"

"I'm already late." Jack pulled the comforter over his head after looking at the clock. "Five more minutes won't make a big difference."

Shaking my head, I finished dressing. I pulled on my favorite sweater for a boost in confidence that I knew I'd need come closing time.

"You must be really tired. Missing me being naked and jumping on you." I yanked the comforter off the bed with a cackle of glee. "Up! Up! Billy made breakfast we can eat on the go!"

Jack's messy hair stood up on end as he glared over his shoulder at me. "Payback. Woman, there will be payback."

Snorting, I placed the comforter on the end of the bed. "Promises, promises." Leaning forward, I gave his ass a quick smack and ran out of the room laughing to his curses.

Billy was plating scrambled eggs as I skidded into the kitchen. He still wore a towel around his waist and his hair was wet. Can I just say yum? His chest hair was so enticing as it led the eyes downward.

"Up here." Billy flicked my nose gently. "None of that until later tonight. I'm only working a half day today, so I can be there when you close up." He passed me a plate with eggs with salt, toast on the side, and the ketchup bottle.

Egg sandwich with ketchup. Perfect. Tasty and easy to eat. I was scooping up the eggs with my fingers onto a piece of the toast when Titus came inside from the front door. He paused when he saw me, his eyes intent on my fingers.

"Cider," his voice was velvety smooth. "Why aren't you using utensils? We don't play with our food." There was a tiny tick in his jaw.

Huh. What do you know? My vampire mate had a pet peeve. Oh, how I would use that, and as often as I could. I should be annoyed with him, but the knowledge it bugged him was worth it.

I offered him a shrug, feigning innocence. "Billy didn't give me a spoon to use with it."

"Hey! Don't blame your heathenness on me!" Billy laughed. He knew how my mind worked. He was well aware that I was already plotting to annoy the hell out of Titus.

I shook the ketchup up, squirting it on the eggs. Titus' nose wrinkled a little and I fought not to laugh. He didn't say anything though.

"This is one of my all time favorite things. Thank you, Billy." I took a very large bite of the egg sandwich, making sure the ketchup pushed over the sides a little bit.

Titus sat at the counter, pulling the bar stool up. His fingers tapped the granite. I could just see the thoughts twirling in his head.

I offered him a bite, holding out the bread to him as the ketchup slowly oozed out of the sides. "Want a bite, sweetie?"

"Err." He pulled back away from it. "No, thank you. I'm full."

"Really?" Lowering my voice in a pout. "You don't like Billy's cooking? You don't want to hurt his feelings, do you?" I fluttered my eyelashes at him as my lower lip trembled.

I could feel Billy next to me. He was doing his best to keep a straight face, but he was shaking a little with how hard he was trying not to move.

"What? I didn't say that!" Titus glanced at Billy. "I enjoyed your food very much. I'm just not a huge ketchup fan."

"Come on." I pushed it closer as I leaned over the counter. "This will change your mind, I promise." My fox's tail was going nuts.

Titus groaned, leaned his head forward and took a bite of the sandwich. Ketchup plopped down onto the countertop as he sat back, chewing slowly with what I could only describe as a panicked look on his face.

Billy wiped up the ketchup without saying a word as we both watched Titus force himself to swallow. He looked like it physically pained him. When he finally swallowed, a soft little noise left him.

That was it. Howling with laughter, my hand slapped the island as I sat the remainder of the sandwich on the plate. Billy was laughing so hard, he was wheezing. He had to hold up his towel with one of his hands.

Titus glanced between us, his lips pressed in a tight line.

"Really?" His tone was so dry, it could peel paint.

That just set Billy and I off again.

When Jack walked in, buttoning his shirt up, he found Billy and I practically on the floor, leaning against each other as we gasped for air. Titus had crossed his arms with a glare that promised revenge in the future.

"Uh?" Jack snagged my sandwich off the plate and finished it in two large bites.

Titus sputtered. "How could you eat that?"

Swallowing, Jack rubbed the back of his hand across his

mouth. "Easy. That was good. You ready to go, baby?" He offered his other hand to me.

I put mine in his and he pulled me into his chest, wrapping his other arm around my waist.

"You'll have to tell me what that was about tonight." He winked down at me as he walked us out the door. "See you two later today!"

The door closed behind us. I felt a little bad for Billy. Leaving him to fend for himself with Titus in a tizzy.

"You're a minx, aren't you?" Jack squeezed my waist.

"Nope. I'm a fox!" I giggled again. "And quite possibly a brat."

"No 'possibly' about it." Jack shook his head as he grinned looking at me. "Life is going to be very interesting with you in it now."

My body melted against his. This guy certainly had a way with words.

"We should get going. We're going to be late." I didn't move from his arms even as I said it, though. "Even if we speed, we're going to be a few minutes late."

"Ah. We're not going to be late. We'll be on time." Jack's confidence was distracting. I wanted to lick his neck.

"Uh, Jack, we have like ten minutes to get there and we haven't moved." My fingers moved along his collar, straightening it. "Can I just say that I really like you in these kinds of shirts?"

His deep rumble warmed me. "I'll make sure to remember that. Now, hold tight." He wrapped his arm around my waist and suddenly, we weren't standing any longer.

Wind surrounded us, our feet left the ground. I squeaked as my hands clutched his shirt.

"Here we go." Jack laughed as we shot forward into the trees like when we'd played tag in the mountains.

"Faster!" My voice rang around us as we sped through the woods toward the rink.

His fingers tightened around me as the wind rushed over and around us. It was a soft, cool caress against my skin. My elation as we flew was something that I would remember for years to come.

CHAPTER 24

I didn't have time to be nervous the rest of the day. As soon as I opened the door, customers streamed in. I ran out of my mixtures, I spent a lot of time going back and forth between the front and back making the drinks.

It was actually a little irritating. I'd gotten a new drink idea while flying through the air with Jack that I wanted to start playing around with. I was even going to name the frosty beverage after him.

I wasn't going to gripe too much. Being busy meant that I was making money with my little store.

Throughout the day, I worked to remember the wall in my mind.

About half way through the day, Neve, a journalist for one of the newspapers in town popped in.

"Hey, Cider." She settled into one of the chairs. "Could I get an original nonalcoholic?" She placed her tablet on the table and rubbed her temples. "I've been trying to get an interview with Darcorp's manager for the past week. There's been rumors that they've been ganging up on a smaller store in the rink. Have you heard anything?"

I finished making her drink, placed it in front of her, and sat down across from her, with my own drink.

"Where'd you hear these rumors?" I took a sip. Man, I made really good drinks.

"Through the grapevine." Neve sighed into her cup. "A journalist can't reveal her sources."

I snorted. I wasn't sure what to tell her. It was probably a good idea to keep everything a secret, at least until Samuel was taken care of.

"I haven't heard anything, but I can keep a look out for you." There. Safe and generic lie.

She narrowed her eyes at me as she continued to sip her drink. "Are you sure? Samuel has been seen coming and going from here over the past few weeks. What should I think of that?"

Tch. My fox admired her cunning all the while our tail twitched in agitation.

"He seems to have taken a liking to my drinks, as has everyone else." Not that I'd ever let him have any, but Neve didn't have to know that.

She finished her drink, brushing her hair over her right shoulder. "I don't believe that, there's a story here, I know it." Neve pushed the empty cup to the middle of the table with some cash. "When you hear something," her smirk was all knowing, "let me have first dibs on it, yeah?"

"I don't know what you're talking about." I had to hand it to her. "But, if I hear anything, you'll be the first one to know."

"That's all I ask. Toodles!" Her fingers wiggled in a wave as she left the store.

I shook my head, grabbed the cups, and went into the back to wash the dirty dishes from the day.

It slowed down significantly after that. I had time to

clean everything, make fresh batches, and even time to start testing the drink that Jack had inspired.

I was having a hard time deciding on the sweetness when an hour to closing rolled around. Billy and Titus arrived, both were having some kind of debate about some kind of sport.

"We'll be right back here during your conversation. When he comes in, we'll let you have your conversation and then come out." Titus kissed the side of my neck. "I promise no maiming."

Igor walked in with Lys, Jack was right behind. Everyone was on time. My mates helped put the chairs up off the floor onto the tables except for one. Igor looked a little off. Her hair was everywhere and she had bags under her eyes.

"Reporting for duty, captain." She saluted cockily.

Apparently, we weren't going to talk about what was wrong.

Later, then.

"Do you have an idea of what you're going to say to him?" Lys grabbed one of my cleaning rags and started to wipe down the back counter on autopilot.

"Not really. I figured on just being blunt. Tell him to get out of Silver Springs." I looked up at Jack as he hugged me from behind.

"It will be in his best interests to leave." Jack ran his hand over the top of my hair. "Igor may not have a chance at him if he upsets you. Keep your wall up."

I kissed his cheek. "Thank you. It'll be okay. I'm pretty sure the idea that the community would come after him for using his powers for evil will be enough to get him out of our rink."

Glancing at the clock, I clapped my hands together. "Okay. Everybody into the back. I've got to get ready."

They all moved in single file through the little curtain that led to the other part of the store. I started making two original ciders. My fox was vibrating with her nerves but, I, on the other hand, was completely calm.

After all that hair pulling worry, to find out that this guy was a supe of a sort and used his powers to mess with my livelihood, I wasn't anxious any longer. I was pissed. For once, though, I was going to work on being diplomatic and not just blow up and escalate the issue. Like I had when Lys had first pranked me.

I should have been mature and confronted her. She'd been angry about her cups that she'd lent me in good faith. When she'd come to inquire about them, I'd been in a terrible mood thanks to the ex. I'd taken it out on her and my brother.

This time, I was going to protect what was mine the right way. No chickens involved. I shuddered involuntarily at the memory.

The clock chimed. Closing time. The door opened right after. Had to give it to the guy. He was prompt.

I faced him with the two mugs. With a mental check on my tree wall in my head, I walked around the counter.

"Thanks for coming, Samuel." I gestured with a hand to the only table not put up for the night. I sat down first, placing the drinks in front of us.

He strode forward confidently, pausing right at the table with a stumble. He corrected himself quickly. If I hadn't been watching him like he was prey, I'd have missed it. Good. He must have realized he wasn't going to mess with me anymore.

"I see that deranged young woman you sent after me

told you what I can do." He smoothed his hands down his shirt. He seemed to do that when he was talking, as if it was an old habit he couldn't kick.

"You're lucky she didn't eat you." I blew on the steam wafting from my mug. "She has a habit of doing that to villains."

Samuel chuckled, his stomach ponch jiggling a little. It wasn't a good look on him. My stomach did the same thing but at least I looked good while it did it.

"I highly doubt that." His hands wrapped around his cup. "Now, why don't we get down to business? The contract is in my office ready for your signature. Hiding your thoughts now won't help you get out of this."

"Yeah, about that." I leaned back, tilting the chair on its back legs. "I'm not going anywhere. Neither is my shop."

Samuel moved his head in disappointment. "That's too bad. This was really the only way that you'd have gotten out of this with some sort of money. Now, I'll just crush your little shop under my boot."

I let a little grin slip out as I reinforced my tree's roots. He wasn't going to see this next part coming.

"On the contrary." My right leg came up and my boot pushed against the edge of the table as I balanced on the chair. "It's you that will be crushed. You see, I don't think you realize what kind of town you've come to reside in."

His brows moved as he frowned. He glanced at my forehead and my lips curled in victory.

"What are you talking about? That you're a shifter? Sure, there's more shifters around here than most places, but that has nothing to do with me." He gripped the edges of his vest, pulling it down tightly twice.

"You really have no clue, do you?" I almost felt sorry for him.

Nah. Not really.

"Silver Springs is a town of supernaturals. Not just shifters, but witches, vampires, trolls, fairies, and man-eating plants that have a deranged personality. How have you been here a few weeks and not noticed?" I sipped my cider, letting it slurp loudly. "What do you think is going to happen when these supes figure out that you've sabotaged one of your own? That you can read minds and use it to fuck people over?"

"Who's going to believe you? It's your word, plus that *thing's* word, against mine. I work for Darcorp Incorporated, one of the top employers in the nation. We're respected and loved. You, on the other hand, are nothing."

Wow, this guy had balls, I'd give him that. He'd just insulted me and Igor without blinking an eye. I really didn't think he knew that Igor would be happy to make him disappear in her stomach.

There was a slight sound from the backroom. I could only imagine it was either Titus or Igor. I would put money on it that the others were keeping them quiet and from coming out here.

Luckily, Samuel was oblivious.

"They'll believe me because I'm part of this wonderful community. There's trust here. You wouldn't know what that meant, even if I took it in a bag of rocks and hit you over the head with it." I held up my hand when he went to open his mouth. "The point is, we will run you out of town, or you will end up in one of the more violent ones' stomach. I suggest that you leave here, you forget my secret recipe, and go settle in another town. Oh, and don't use your powers for evil."

"You are a fool. I will crush you. I will crush your friends. You will beg me by the end to work for me when no one else will hire you. And when that happens, I will graciously give you the lowest job and make you grateful for it."

The guy just started to laugh. He didn't believe me. I sighed. Enough was enough. I stood, walked around the table, and while looking down at the scum infested man, grew my claws and with sufficient force stabbed down into his thigh, right next to his little balls.

As he let out a painful whimper, my mates came out from the back room with Lys and Igor. They all had varying expressions. If it wasn't such a serious situation, I'd have laughed at them.

Titus gently reached for my arm, pulling my nails out, patting my hand. His eyes were on Samuel's face. His eyes promised death. I threaded our fingers together and squeezed, getting his attention back to me.

"I think it's in your best interest to listen to my mate." Titus' voice was hard, scary. It only turned me on.

I had issues.

"She just stabbed me!" Samuel whined as he clutched his thigh.

"It's just a little stab. Nothing fatal." Igor leaned forward, tilting her head as she sniffed the air close to him. "Pity. If she'd stabbed a little bit higher, it could have been fatal."

Samuel's skin paled more than it already was. He glanced between all of us surrounding him. "You're all insane." Pushing out his chair, he stumbled backward, away from all of us. "You won't get away with this."

"I think she will." Titus stepped in front of all of us, his back blocking my view. "I think you'll take her advice and leave town. Tonight. Igor will be happy to escort you out."

He nodded to her as she came to stand next to him, her crazy grin sending a shiver of fear down my spine.

Oh, crap. This wasn't the plan.

"Titus." My hand touched his back. "We discussed this."

"We did. We tried it your way. He's just too dense to seem to understand that you were trying to help him. I'm not going to stand by while he is here and thinks he can hurt you." Titus didn't even look back at me.

Billy, next to me, wrapped his arm around my shoulder. "Let them do this. This guy has a black soul and isn't worth the time you've wasted on him."

"What are you idiots talking about? I'm standing right here! Move! I need to get to a hospital," Samuel sputtered loudly.

"Yes, let's show this fly out." Igor's glee was apparent and I felt a little squeamish. She really wasn't planning on eating him, was she?

"Wait. Igor. Titus. Come on. We just want him to go away and forget about my recipe. That's it." I glanced between them. Jack came up to my other side and wrapped his arm around my waist.

"Cider," Igor offered me a sweet look, "I won't do anything to upset you. You've been kind to me, been my friend. Let me take this man away from here. I won't cause him pain. Besides, this gives me the excuse to explore more of the world, yes?" She gripped Samuel's arm and proceeded to drag him out of the store. "You'll have to get another part time worker. Sorry! Let's pick up some steak sauce on the way out of town, yes?" The door closed behind them as Samuel struggled against Igor's unnaturally strong grip. The shop was quiet for several long moments.

"Well, that went way off kilter." Lys slapped her hands

together in mirth. "I am going to head home. Jace is off tonight and promised to give me a lap dance. He got a new piercing, so I can't wait to play with it."

Titus winced. "Really? Did you have to tell us that? I'm standing right here."

She laughed as she left. "That's what you get, DAD."

Titus looked at us in confusion. "What did I do?"

Shaking my head, I leaned into my other two mates. "Who knows?" Then, it suddenly hit me. All the stress melted away and my legs gave out. Jack's arm tightened to keep me up. "It's over. It's really over." Whatever Igor planned to do to Samuel meant that I got to keep my shop and business. "This whole thing has been crazy, but there is one thing that I'm thankful for." I touched Jack's cheek. "I have my mates."

EPILOGUE

"Damnit, Cider!" Billy groaned. "Why must you tease me?" His panting whine was adorable.

I licked the tip, the cream was delicious. I kept a firm grip on the base.

"It's not my fault that I was faster." I bit down on the popsicle. "Damn, it's so good and creamy."

Billy wiped his brow, glaring at me from where he laid across the couch. "You're a jerk."

"I asked yesterday if we were running low on anything when I was at the grocery store. Not my fault." This time I sang out my reply. "It's sooooo good."

His middle finger went up in reply as I cackled from the island.

"Long day?" My legs swung on the barstool.

"Titus is a cruel customer. I was excited to take over the contract of landscaping his place, but damn, he wanted it just right and I wasn't allowed to leave until it was just so. He's so lucky he gives good head." Billy tipped his head back with his eyes closed.

"Ah, my poor Billy goat." I hopped off the stool and

leaned over the edge of the couch, pressing the side of the popsicle to his mouth. "I'll share."

His tongue swiped out, finishing the remainder of the tasty treat in one bite. I wasn't even upset. He dropped the wooden stick onto the table and pulled me over the edge. I laughed as I fell on top of him.

"Well, I think knowing Titus is even more OCD than you are is pretty adorable. Do you see how twitchy he gets when he sees my room?" My chin rested on his chest.

"That is fun." His large hand moved down my back to my ass. "I like the way Jack just doesn't care either way. He does have a tendency to be on your side, though."

I giggled. "He really just wants us all happy. He knows when I'm happy, you guys tend to be."

His big shoulders shrugged. "I'm looking forward to my date with him later this week. Think he'll take me to the ice rink?" His hand ran along my thigh, making me shiver.

"I want details, wherever you guys go. Especially if it means you two do the naughty tango."

My mates were enjoying each other just as much as I enjoyed them.

It'd been a little over a month since the confrontation against Samuel. Igor was gone. She'd left a note with Iris, telling her that she wanted to explore the world and learn how to be the best version she could be without compromising herself. I'd hired one of the older teens from the orphanage in town as her replacement. So far, everything was going great with them.

No one had heard from Samuel. It was about a week later that the construction on the building for Darcorp stopped and it disappeared one night. As if a sudden, unexplainable snow storm had torn it apart and scattered the rubble.

Things were going more smoothly with Quinten. He was still a little sensitive if I joked about blue balls, but it seemed to amuse Lys to no end.

We were working on becoming friends. It wasn't happening overnight, but it was a slow process. We've met up for goat yoga at Maya's twice so far.

Titus and Jack stayed at our house a few times a week. They both had multiple drawers at this point in both Billy's and my rooms. I was hoping that in a few more months, we could ask them just to move in permanently with us.

I looked down at my best friend. So many things had changed since that day I went skating after work. Falling in love with each of them was just the icing on the cake.

I pressed our lips together in a chaste kiss.

Who knows what the future holds for us? All I knew was that whatever came our way, we'd all face it together.

And sex. There would be lots of sex.

The End. For Now. Maybe. Who knows?
The Panda Overlords are fickle things.

NEVE BY HELEN SCOTT:
HTTPS://BOOKS2READ.COM/NEVE

When I'm dropped off in a little podunk town called Silver Springs under orders from my jerk of a father to turn their human newspaper from a money pit into a profitable business I want to scream. After meeting the sexy journalist that works there, a demon stripper, a reindeer shifter, and a selkie, they'll have me screaming for a whole different reason. I'm Neve and I'm the city girl who hated Silver Springs until my mates thawed my icy heart.

KARI BY ELENA GRAY: HTTPS://MYBOOK.TO/KARI

House sitting for Willow was supposed to be easy and fun. Instead, someone's playing tricks on me and I keep ending up naked in strange places with hot guys. And not just normal men, but a brooding god of the underworld, an 18th century Highlander and a swoon-worthy dragon shifter - although maybe that's not so bad. I'm Kari, and with all these sexy men around me, I'm sure to get my happily every after - aren't I?

STORM BY EVA DELANEY

My mates shift into dicks, throw their cocks around, lie to grow their penises... and raise hamburgers from the dead. I'm Storm, and my life has turned into chaos just when I need to save Silver Springs. It's a good thing I'm a raptor shifter, because detachable dicks and zombie cows ain't gonna cut it.

EIRWEN BY JEWELS ARTHUR

Freedom and dick, that's all I really want in life. First, I need to escape my ice-dicked fiancé and get to Silver Springs, a land of magical dildos where paranormal creatures run free. Then I need to find some sexy men to defile me in the dirtiest ways possible. Pound town, here comes Eirwen.

EIRLYS BY JENN D. YOUNG: HTTPS://BOOKS2READ.COM/EIRLYS

What do coffee, a manwhore incubus, a tender red fox, and a reclusive foxy artist have in common? Oh right. Me. Watch out for crazy pranks involving chickens, pussy glitter and blue dicks. But don't be fooled. Triple E will reign supreme and we will crush Cider. I'm Eirlys, get your caffeine ready and buckle up for the insane ride I'm gonna take you on.

CIDER BY ASPEN BLACK

The prank wars have ended. Of course, I was the winner. Regardless of what that vampire thinks. Hot Ciders' Snack Bar is the place to be. Until *they* start to move in, putting every store at the rink in risk.
Not to mention that I've acquired three mates, including Eirlys daddy vamp.
I'm Cider and this is the story of my survival.
mybook.to/CiderSilverSkates

FROSTINE BY J.E. CLUNEY

I moved to Silver Springs to enjoy a quiet life away from my family who wished for me to take a mate of their choosing. Sadly, there's no running from my family, and they send two potential suitors out to fetch me.
Throw in the broody ice-phoenix who has fallen for me, and things are about to get heated. I'm Frostine, and things are about to get hot.

PEPPERMINT BY CALI MANN: HTTPS://BOOKS2READ.COM/PEPPERMINT

I'm just a cardinal shifter, and they are three fierce warriors. But when they're trapped in the underworld by Loki's curse, I'll do anything I can to save them, even armed only with a pair of ice skates and a letter. I'm Peppermint, and I'm a mail carrier, a klutzy bird shifter, and reluctant messenger to the dead.

CANDELA BY J.R. THORN

What do a firefighter, a Fire Fae, and a husky shifter have in common? They all want a bite of Candela's cupcake.

MISTY BY TABITHA BARRET

I was happy dating emotionally unavailable men, especially after being rejected by my merc for hire mate, but now I'm reconsidering that after a night of body shots with my beastie's off-limits conjurer brother and hearing the passionate singing voice of the sexy funeral director. Should I break the rules so I can find my happiness or should I keep running from my past? I'm Misty, aka Gray, Silver Spring's second favorite tattoo artist.

ICLYN BY MELISSA ADAMS: BLACKLISTED IN ALL OF HOLLYWOOD, I NEED A JOB AND A PLACE TO STAY.

Maybe my luck is about to change as I get hired as a photographer for the Silver Springs On Ice beauty pageant. I have to re-learn how to ice skate but it's like riding a bike, right?
I'm staying in a haunted B&B and I have the hots for my new boss and his annoying bodyguard. I'm Iclyn and I'm royally screwed.
http://mybook.to/IclynSilverSkates14

AURORA BY M.J. MARSTENS

I don't believe in witches, spells, fated mates--and I sure as hell don't believe in ice skating! I hate anything to do with cold weather and snow. *Nothing* is making *me* visit Silver Springs. . . I'm AURORA and this is my shitcicle of story.

LUMI BY CRYSTAL NORTH

New to town, running my own business, single mom...life can be super hard. Add in magical powers that, even in a town as accommodating as Silver Springs, I need to keep on the down low, and a daughter who's emerging powers are causing havoc, and I've got my hands full. Love? No thank you. Love x3? Hell no! *I'm Lumi and this is my story of how fate has other ideas for me.*

Join the Spell Library fan club for exclusive advanced access to books, plus weekly giveaways and games.

Want to receive news about Silver Springs? Subscribe to the Silver Springs Herald!

But wait! There's more on the next page!

ASPEN BLACK'S BOOKS

Loved Cider? Why not take a look at other books by

Aspen Black

Standalone

Shrouded In The Dark

The Ghost Dud Series

Ghost Revelations

Ghost Deceptions

Ghost Confessions

Ghost Transformations

EXCALIBUR'S DECISION SERIES: ARYANA'S
JOURNEY

The Silver Springs Library Series

Book can be read as a standalone

Iris Book 9

Silver Skates

Book can be read as a standalone

Cider Book 8

*Secrets of Talonsville Charity Series (%50 of
proceeds are donated to charity)*

Knight's Talons

Please visit Aspen and her co-author's group on Facebook

Aspen Black and Adammeh's Wanderers

Printed in Great Britain
by Amazon